ANY WHICH WAY YOU CAN

'Hey Beddoe – it's us!'

Philo turned his head. The entire Black Widow gang were strung out across the width of the road to his right – in a long and intimidating line. At least they would have been intimidating, Philo considered, if they had not consisted of the stupidest, greasiest, most slack-jawed sons of bitches this side of Alaska. He sighed, recalling a series of farcical incidents the previous summer during which he had single-handedly and with minimal effort disposed of most of the Black Widow bike fleet.

ANY WHICH WAY YOU CAN

novelisation by Gerald Cole

from the screenplay by Stanford Sherman

and based on characters created by
Jeremy Joe Kronsberg

Star

A STAR BOOK

published by
the Paperback Division of
W. H. ALLEN & Co. Ltd

A Star Book
Published in 1982
by the Paperback Division of
W. H. Allen & Co. Ltd
A Howard and Wyndham Company
44 Hill Street, London W1X 8LB

Photoset by V & M Graphics Ltd, Aylesbury, Bucks
Printed in Great Britain by
Hunt Barnard Printing Ltd, Aylesbury, Bucks

ISBN 0 352 310405

CHAPTER ONE

A hot wind straight from the Mojave Desert fanned across the old Route 66. Its blast seemed to set the unfolding blacktop writhing even more frenziedly in the afternoon heat haze. The scorched grasslands, speeding by on either side, appeared to darken to a dimmer shade of brown.

'Ooweeee,' mouthed Orville Boggs, shifting his grip on the wheel of the battered Chevy Apache pick-up, and wishing he'd brought sunglasses. 'Sure is sticky.'

Philo Beddoe smiled quietly. 'Clyde likes it,' he offered. The large red-haired orang-utan, sitting urbanely by the nearside window, turned sad eyes on his best buddy and smacked his lips affectionately.

Orville chuckled and shook his head. He was an easy-going, clown-faced man of about thirty-five, with a perpetual look of wary innocence and a peaked mechanic's cap that only left his head in the shower, and sometimes not even then. If Clyde was happy with the heat, he wasn't going to argue.

He reached down to scratch his rump, feeling the bulge of dollar bills in the back pocket of his jeans. At the same moment two California Highway Patrolmen zipped past, erect and resplendent on their gleaming Electra Glides. Orville watched them draw ahead down the blacktop and his expression darkened. 'I don't know, Philo,' he said. 'Takin' on a cop – '

Philo squinted through the windshield. 'Well, one thing's for sure,' he said. 'This is one fight that ain't gonna get busted.'

Philo's bareknuckle prowess was legendary from San Francisco to the Gulf of Mexico. There was always someone only too glad to put it to the test – and still others climbing over each other to wager money on the outcome. Just like today.

Orville raised doubtful eyebrows and clicked his teeth.

His respect for the law largely consisted of keeping it at a decent arm's length on every possible occasion. Frowning, he watched the two patrolmen climb a slight rise in the road ahead and dissolve in the shimmering heat. There was unusual activity on Route 66 that afternoon. Trucks, trailers and heavy rigs which would normally have never strayed from the newer, faster interstates had developed a sudden preference for the once famous east-west highway. CHiP patrols had increased massively, though the official radio channels seemed less concerned with reports of crime than a vigorous debating of odds. CB chatter joined in the general discussion and soon the air waves were crackling.

At a steady fifty-five miles an hour this garrulous motor armada sped beyond the Los Angeles city limits and out into the sun-baked hinterland of San Bernadino.

There was a shared excitement among the travellers, a baiting cameraderie which the CHiP men tolerated grudgingly.

Accelerating down a long straight stretch of highway, the two motorcycle patrolmen who had passed Philo and Orville overtook a heavy two-horned tractor-trailer and settled back to just below the legal speed limit twenty yards in front of it. Slowly the huge vehicle edged up behind them, until a sudden blast from both horns sent both motorcycles wobbling out the way.

Inside the cab a grizzled trucker gave a cheery wave as the rig steamed ahead. One of the patrolmen fell back beside the trucker's open window.

'How'd you like to have your goddam rig impounded?' he shrieked over the diesel roar.

The driver smiled engagingly. 'Sorry, Officer,' he bellowed. 'My hand slipped.'

Scowling, the officer wrenched on the throttle.

Five miles down the road another motorcycle patrolman was enduring the taunts of a gang of men clinging precariously to the sides of a lumber truck.

'Hey!' yelled one. 'You better get ready to hock your tricycle, Jack!'

'Yeah?' snarled the patrolman, drawing alongside. 'Let's see your money, big mouth!'

Leaning out dangerously, the truck rider thrust a handful of bills in the officer's face. 'Two hundred on Philo!' he bawled. 'You're covered!' the policeman snapped and accelerated away from a burst of derisive laughter.

In the distance the dust-white silos and conveyors of a cement factory reared against the sky. In its shadow a circle of heavy rigs, parked tractor to trailer, marked the collective destination. Orville turned toward it down a narrow dirt road. Churning dust, a CHiP patrol car preceded him. At the far end a motorcycle cop and a whistling trucker were dividing the traffic.

The Apache was directed to a spot beside a rig. Cheers and cries of recognition went up as the milling crowd caught sight of Philo. He swapped glances with Orville. There had to be well over a hundred people here; it was going to be a profitable afternoon for someone.

The pick-up shuddered to a halt and they piled out. Despite the dust and the heat there was a sharp sense of urgency in the air. Knots of excited men formed and re-formed, shouting the odds here, making a bargain there; crumpled single bills and smoothly folded wads changed hands on every side.

As Philo lifted Clyde onto the tailboard of the pick-up, Orville spotted the man he was looking for.

'I'll go handle this,' he murmured.

Philo nodded and began to drag his sweatshirt over his head. Orville moved across the field to a squat, bald-headed trucker who was counting dollars from a black patrolman. 'Put all of it on him,' urged the officer, stabbing a finger at a nearby cluster of fawn-uniformed CHiP men. In the middle of them, jogging on the spot, was a heavy, grim-faced man in a vest. The United States Marine Corps legend was tattooed conspicuously on his upper arm. Orville eyed him speculatively.

'Twelve hundred dollars,' he told the bald man, counting them out.

7

'Twelve hundred,' the trucker acknowledged, nodding to a helper, who scribbled it down.

With another glance at the jogger, Orville moved back toward the pick-up.

'Cooley!' the bald man yelled at the CHiP contingent. 'I've got twelve hundred more on Philo!'

Police Sergeant Aloysius Cooley, a sour-mouthed, hard-bitten Irishman in his early fifties, nodded and growled in reply:

'You're covered!'

He ducked his head to a young patrolman at his side. 'You know, we're coverin' over eight thousand dollars here so far.' Officer Morgan grinned confidently. 'We'll eat 'im for breakfast. Hell, Joe whipped every marine in the first division.'

He threw a warm glance at the rippling shoulders of the jogger in front of him. Officer Joe Casey - the CHiP contestant - aimed a selection of jabs at a phantom opponent. Sergeant Cooley followed Morgan's gaze, and grunted.

Philo had a reputation for bypassing the law if the mood took him and it would please the sergeant mightily to take him down a peg. But sometimes Casey seemed just a little too eager.

'Yeah,' said Cooley, lifting his gaze to Philo and Orville who were standing by their pick-up. 'But Beddoe ain't a marine.'

'Jesus,' murmured Orville, staring back across the makeshift arena. 'He's big.'

From a distance Casey seemed not to have shrunk an inch in size or impressiveness. He was easily Philo's height, but without the latter's rangy, athletic build; Casey had more of the quality of a solid brick wall.

'Yeah,' agreed Philo, bending to tie a training shoe. 'He's sizeable.'

Orville looked at him. 'They said he beat everybody in the Marine Corps.'

Philo straightened up and flexed an arm muscle. 'Well,' he said, 'I ain't a marine.'

8

The bald trucker flashed a grin full of teeth at Sergeant Cooley.

'I got twenty-eight hundred from the boys in Bakersfield!' he yelled.

Cooley frowned and glanced over his shoulder. A few yards behind him, discreetly aloof, his captain leaned against a parked patrol car. The man nodded curtly over dark glasses. Cooley turned back to the trucker. 'You're covered!' he shouted, and sighed. That was nearly three thousand dollars riding on the personal guarantee of his immediate superior. He tapped Casey on the shoulder. 'You know, you lose this fight an' we'll be patrollin' Death Valley for the next five years.'

'Don't worry about it, Sarge,' Officer Morgan piped in, nudging Casey. 'Eat 'im up, Joe!'

Taking his cue, a grinning Casey shadow-boxed his way into the centre of the field. A cheer went up from the crowd; it began to tighten into a circle.

'Take care o' Clyde, will ya?' Philo asked Orville. 'You know how he likes t' crap in squad cars.'

'Yeah,' murmured Orville, moving closer to the tailboard. The great ape blinked at him mildly. Affable as Clyde was, he had a habit of causing more than his fair share of social embarrassment.

Fresh cheers arose as Philo took a deep breath and stepped into the makeshift ring. From its farther side Casey regarded him coldly. The two men began to circle, sizing each other up. A gloating look came into Casey's face. Philo was tall but stringy; men like that just didn't have the weight to make a punch count; Casey had flattened dozens like this one. He felt a surge of confidence.

Philo allowed himself no such luxury. The raw red anger that could transform the least of his punches into the equivalent of a sideswipe from a heavy breaker lurked well below the surface of his mind. The topmost levels were cold, clear and very busy.

Casey was a bully; it showed in his eyes and the petulant twist to his lips. This was a man who liked more than

9

anything else to be on top, and if he wasn't he was likely to lash out without too much clear thought.

Observation number two: he was big and he was heavy, but a lot of that weight looked like fat. If he'd been a big shot in the marines, he'd also spent the last year sitting pretty in a squad car and a few last minute physical jerks weren't going to overcome that.

In seconds, Philo had his strategy worked out: move fast, punch to hurt so that Casey lost his temper and started to slog; let him tire, then - in for the kill.

Abruptly Casey lunged, loosing a lightening fast right that only even swifter footwork from Philo saved from shattering his jaw. So much for strategy, he thought, feeling the draught of Casey's fist against his temple.

But the suspicion of fat hadn't been wrong. Everything Casey had had gone into that abortive blow and he spun awkwardly, momentarily off-balanced. Phil smacked two rapid-fire punches into the side of his head. Shouts of delight burst from the truckers.

Gasping, Casey recovered, rounding on Philo. Two less violent blows followed, one to the head which Philo blocked easily with his forearm, and another to the mid-section, landing hard enough to make Philo grunt. Cheers thundered from the CHiP men.

Suddenly everyone seemed to be shouting at the same time, bellowing encouragement or abuse, mimicking each piledriver blow.

The excitement was too much for Orville. Already the crowd had blocked off his view of the battle. He turned quickly to Clyde. 'Hold it! Hold it!' he warned, and pushed through the milling bodies.

As he reached the edge of the ring the two fighters began to exchange punches rapidly. Casey was slogging, swinging with a brutal strength that made Orville wince. Philo was ducking most of them and more of his shorter, sharper jabs were striking home, but they only seemed to sting Casey, annoying rather than rocking him back.

'OK Joe! All right! All right!' bellowed an officer at Orville's side.

'He's killin' 'im! He's killin' 'im!' shrieked Officer Morgan, across the ring.

Immediately three sharp jabs from Philo sent Casey reeling backward.

'He's movin' pretty good for a corpse,' commented Cooley. He began to think darkly of his pension.

In the back of the pick-up Clyde grew bored. Noisy crowds didn't bother him – he'd experienced enough of those in Philo's company. He'd dozed off on the drive down, so he didn't feel sleepy. He'd even exhausted the pick-up's supply of bananas. No, some new source of stimulation was needed. He shuffled to the tailboard and swung himself down to the ground. Ignored by the excited crowd, he ambled towards the nearest rig, snuffling quietly to himself, his long, prehensile arms grazing the dirt. Catching hold of an inspection ladder at the rear of the trailer, he climbed swiftly to the metal roof.

Below, in a circle of vociferous human beings, Philo seemed occupied. Clyde regarded him solemnly a moment then looked away. A short way off, round the circle of parked rigs, he caught sight of a blue and white saloon. The CHiP shield on the driver's door stirred a pleasurable memory in the back of Clyde's mind.

Grunting, he set off in a rolling, long-armed lope along the roof of the trailer, his bowels twitching in anticipation.

Philo tasted blood.

He could sense its salt tang in his mouth, feel its heat pumping through his veins in surges of mounting, over-ripe joy. Each blow that Casey landed – fewer and wilder as his tiredness showed – only swelled his excitement. The kill was close.

Angry, aching for just one pile-driver to slam home, Casey threw a wide, curving right at Philo's head. Philo backstepped easily. His left jabbed forward, catching his opponent squarely in his exposed gut. He grunted and doubled up. Philo's right came rocketing upwards from

11

below his waist. It connected neatly with Casey's jaw. Glassy-eyed, he staggered backwards, fought vainly for balance and crashed onto one knee, his head falling.

The crowd roared.

Panting, Philo moved in, waiting for Casey to rise. Then cheers more shrill than the others fell oddly on his ears, distracting him. He looked up. Two stetsoned teeny-boppers, leaping up and down, shrieked enthusiasm for him at the ringside. Beneath their skintight tee-shirts two pairs of generous bosoms bobbed in intriguing rhythms. An appreciative smile came to Philo's lips.

A fraction of a second before Casey's bunched fist. Shooting back to his feet, Casey aimed a second blow at Philo's midriff, slicing fiercely.

Stunned, Philo lurched back.

'Bingo!' yelled Officer Morgan.

Anger flared in Philo's eyes as he realised his carelessness. There was a smirk on Casey's face. He staggered forward, still half winded by his last effort at recovery. And Philo let his anger take him.

Two hammer blows to left and right cheek wrenched Casey's head in opposite directions. As he gasped for breath, Philo slashed at his stomach, once, twice, thrice: a vicious tattoo. Casey stumbled and a final right swung out of the sun, clubbing him to his knees once more. He hung there, fighting for breath, unable to raise his head.

Philo stepped back.

'All right, that's it!' he announced.

'Well he ain't down yet!' came Morgan's protest.

Philo rounded on him, his anger still hot. 'No, he ain't down an' I ain't puttin' 'im down. Of course, if you wanna take 'is place, we c'n arrange that!'

Without waiting for a reply, he stomped off through the crowd. Morgan stared after him, open-mouthed.

'The fight ain't over till 'e's down!' he bellowed.

Sergeant Cooley, who was helping other officers drag a befuddled Casey to his feet, threw him a look of disgust.

'Shuddup!' he hissed.

'How much did we pull down?' Philo asked Orville as

they reached the pick-up.

Around them the crowd was breaking up. Diesel engines sparked and rattled into action.

'Twelve hundred,' said Orville, pushing the thick wad into his back pocket. Philo nodded and wiped a trickle of blood off his mouth. He glanced in the empty cab of the pick-up and turned back abruptly.

'Where's Clyde?' he snapped.

Orville raised despairing eyes skyward. 'Oh, shhhhhit!'

Philo looked round quickly. 'There he is,' he spoke in an undertone. The great ape bowled towards them, skirting the parked semis. There was a glow of satisfaction in his deep, watery eyes. Directly behind him was the CHiP squad car, its driver's door ajar.

A CHiP captain was striding towards it, then paused to talk to another officer.

'Clyde,' hissed Philo, grasping the ape's hairy hand and guiding him swiftly into the pick-up cab. 'You got damn little respect for the law!'

Clyde blew a resonant raspberry.

'God,' whispered Orville, sliding in beside them.

Philo twisted the ignition, gunned the engine and turned rapidly towards the exit. Across the field the captain's nostrils twitched. There was a distinct hint of dung in the air, though he hadn't noticed any livestock in the vicinity. Dismissing it, he pulled open the door to his car. A dark, spreading mass was piled high in the driver's seat. Then the full stench of Clyde's keepsake struck him squarely in the nose.

'Sergeant Cooley!' the captain bellowed.

Fifty yards away down the dirt road, Orville breathed easier as the Apache neared the highway. He glanced in the rear mirror. The first of the heavy rigs was raising dust as it wheeled out of the field. That should hold back any vengeful patrolmen for a minute or two.

Relaxing, he looked back at Philo, and grew curious. There was an unusually sombre air about his buddy. Philo normally emerged from a fight with the kind of inner glow more peaceable men reserved for a successful

13

seduction. This afternoon's victory seemed to have left him quite unmoved. Orville knew better than to ask questions. If Philo felt any need to unburden himself he'd do it in his own good time.

That time came almost at once.

As the pick-up slowed for the highway junction, Philo announced impassively, 'This is gonna be my last fight.'

Orville gaped at him in astonishment. He hadn't expected anything as drastic as this.

'How come?' he snapped.

Philo glanced up and down the highway. 'Right turn, Clyde,' he ordered. The orang-utan shot a hairy fist through the open nearside window. Philo pulled out onto the blacktop and turned west.

'I'm gettin' t' like the pain,' he said.

Orville stared at him, waiting for more. Nothing came. He stretched his eyebrows, shaking his head. He'd always assumed Philo simply weathered the discomfort for the greater good of beating his opponent to a pulp. He could imagine how enjoying the discomfort for its own sake could disturb a man. But to throw up bouts that earned him twelve hundred dollars in four and a half minutes ...

'Well,' said Orville dubiously, 'I guess it's time then.'

'Yeah, I think,' said Philo, staring fixedly ahead.

Sergeant Cooley gripped the wheel of the captain's car, his battered face working into fresh configurations of ugliness as he tried to conquer the overpowering effect of Clyde's depradations and still steer a straight line down the highway. His thoughts were as fetid as the atmosphere in the saloon. Getting bawled out in public by the captain was one thing, being ordered to scoop shit out of his car was quite another. What kind of foul-minded maniac could have done such a thing? Whoever he was, he obviously had a stomach problem of staggering proportions.

'I don't understand it,' wailed Joe Casey from the back seat. 'I whipped every marine in my division! Some real tough guys.'

'Oh Jesus,' gasped Cooley. 'How can you stand the

stench?' Casey blinked at him in the rear mirror, his nose already bloated from Philo's last onslaught.

'I can't smell nothin',' he said.

Fifty yards up the highway, Orville was still brooding over Philo's sudden announcement. On an impulse he rummaged in the cluttered shelf under the dash. Tucked down the back was a crumpled paper bag. He dredged it out and unearthed a half squashed banana Clyde had missed on the drive out. Orville bit off the good end and immediately found himself under intense scrutiny from the great ape. Sighing, Orville handed over the remainder.

'The Captain won't transfer us, will he, Sarge?' queried Officer Morgan. Seated next to Cooley, he gave the Sergeant a look of pathetic hope.

'Seein' as how we flushed twenty-eight hundred of 'is hard earned bucks ...' Cooley snarled, and shook his head. 'Ohhh, it's Death Valley, son. You c'n believe me.'

'Some *real* tough guys,' burbled Casey from the back.

Ahead in the Apache, Clyde vacuumed the last of the squashed banana, smacked his lips appreciatively and tossed the empty skin out of the window. Caught in the slipstream it arced high in the air, turned over and splatted on the windshield of the following squad car. 'Hey!' cried Morgan, straining forward. 'Pull those guys over. They're littering!'

Sergeant Cooley's eyes slitted; his mouth became a rigid line as breath eased through his nostrils.

'Will you just ...' he began softly. Then he exploded. 'Shuddup, will ya!'

CHAPTER 2

Anthony Paoli's long, black, shaded glass limousine left his family's New Jersey stronghold at noon and drove straight to Manhattan via the Holland Tunnel. Once on the Island it detoured right towards the Battery, gliding to a halt outside a nondescript brownstone at the back of Canal Street.

While Anthony sat stiffly in the cushioned rear seat, one of his two elegantly suited companions slipped out the car and moved briskly up the front steps, glancing to left and right as he went.

Within thirty seconds he was back, a small grey box under his arm. Climbing into the car, he handed it to Anthony. The dark-haired young man examined it carefully. It was about a foot square, made of perforated aluminium, with a carrying handle on top. Anthony released a bolt on the lid and cracked it open. From inside came a snort of breath and the scuffling sound of claws on metal.

Smiling, Anthony nodded to the man who brought it. With a soft purr, the limo swept away from the kerb.

It moved into Broadway, skirting Greenwich Village and turning off into Fifth Avenue as it reached the theatre district.

It was just after one that it halted once more, outside a towering apartment block in East 86th Street with an oblique and very expensive view of Central Park.

Flanked by his companions, and with a firm grip on the aluminium box, Anthony moved into the foyer and announced himself.

He was shown straight to the lift which whisked all three men to the sixth floor.

An English-style butler opened the door to James Beekman's apartment. Anthony Paoli stepped inside, sweeping the aluminium box away from the butler's

16

proferred grasp. There was deep-piled carpet underfoot, carefully graded marble on the hallway walls, with ceiling-high mirrors at intervals. A buzz of animated conversation came from an inner room.

Anthony sniffed. As the son and heir of one of New York's best established Dons, he felt free to look askance at a man like Beekman. An English butler and a hundred tons of imported marble couldn't disguise the fact that Beekman had clawed his way out of the Bronx on nothing. Just luck, *chutzpah* and a reckless desire to cover bets no sane businessman would touch with a pole.

One slip and tomorrow he'd be back at the bottom of the heap. Anthony smiled inwardly. With what he had in the box, it could be today.

The butler ushered him forward into the drawing room. It was bright, plushly furnished and crowded. A waist-high open topped glass tank stood in the middle of the carpet. A crumpled sack, tied with string, lay in the bottom of it.

'May I take your wager, sir?' the butler began, but Anthony simply raised three fingers and swept past, stopping at the tank.

He looked balefully across at Beekman and his lieutenant Patrick Scarfe who were chatting amiably with others in the party.

'Pardon me, sir,' said the butler, scuttling behind him. 'Was that, uh, three thousand?'

Anthony stared hard at Beekman. 'No, it is not three thousand,' he snapped.

The butler coughed and glanced at his employer. 'Mr Paoli bets thirty thousand on the challenger,' he announced.

Beekman nodded and smiled easily at Anthony. He was a heavy, sweating man in his mid-forties with a liking for shiny suits and substantial male jewellery. While the butler noted Anthony's bet in a note book, Beekman motioned to Scarfe and approached the side of the tank. The others in the room gathered round, conversation falling away. The butler slipped his note book inside his

17

jacket and joined Anthony at the tank side. The younger man was still staring at Beekman, who now nodded.

Anthony lifted the aluminium box over the side of the tank and deposited it on the bottom next to the tied sack. Reaching both hands down, he released the bolt on the lid and tipped the box sideways. A narrow furry head with bright, beady eyes peeped out. Then a lean, bushy-tailed body squirmed free. As Anthony pulled the box away, the mongoose skittered round the tank, finally stopping and sniffing curiously at the sack.

Now the butler reached down. As the spectators leaned forward, he gripped a loose end of string with one hand and gingerly plucked at a corner of the sack with the other. In one swift movement he jerked the string loose and whisked the sack away.

With a shrill rattle, a green-scaled, fully grown rattlesnake dropped on to the tank floor, its head twisting and rising.

Instinctively the spectators jerked back; a couple gasped. Beekman laughed and flashed a glance at Anthony who looked pale. The snake was a monster. Anthony did not know that Beekman had had an animal dealer in Fort Worth scouring the Mid West for the biggest, meanest example of its kind for the past two months.

The mongoose began circling, its eyes fixed on the rattler's gently swaying head. Halfway round the tank, the snake struck, its whole body jerking forward. The mongoose leapt into the air, twisting sideways as it fell, and darting at the serpent's outstretched head. Grazed by needle sharp teeth, the snake jerked back. The mongoose sprang forward, snapping beneath the serpent's jaws. With a lightning swift movement, the snake kissed the exposed back of its attacker's neck. The contact lasted fractions of a second.

'Ha!' Beekman cried. 'That's it! That's it!'

The spectator's looked at him in astonishment. The mongoose was still circling.

Anthony Paoli's face contorted into anger. 'He never touched 'im!'

Beekman shook his head, his smile fading. 'Your animal's gonna be dead in fifteen seconds!'

Anthony started forward, his companions bristling on either side.

Patrick Scarfe moved in front of Beekman. 'Young man ...' he warned.

'Keep your terrier in his cage, Beekman!' Anthony snapped. But he halted. He glanced into the tank. The mongoose was shaking its head; it retreated against the glass.

'Junior,' said Beekman reasonably, 'he's only lookin' out for my interest, that's all.'

Anthony's expression soured as he recognised defeat. It was not a feeling he knew well or enjoyed.

Stony-faced, he said, 'Your money'll be here by five p.m.'

Beekman shrugged expansively. 'I expected no less.'

With a scowl Anthony Paoli turned and swept out, flanked by his companions. The butler draped a sheet over the tank where the snake curled quietly, inches from the dead mongoose. The party broke up swiftly.

Only as the last guest departed, did a jubilant Beekman give himself up to laughter. 'Wooo - eee!' he cried, snatching up a Jack Daniels and sprawling on the sofa. He chuckled again at the memory of Anthony Paoli's face.

How he'd relished taking that sucker for a ride. Without his father or his money, a punk like that wouldn't last ten minutes where Beekman had come from.

Then he reminded himself who Anthony's father was. It didn't pay to offend the Paoli clan. He'd find a way to make amends, which of course would put young Anthony's nose out even further.

'Hey!' he turned to Scarfe, who settled beside him. 'Did you set up a fight for Wilson?'

Scarfe shook his head and sipped at his glass. 'No, not yet.' He was small and spry with Beekman's background but an accountant's head for figures.

The larger man's mood changed abruptly.

'Well, c'monn - ' He spread his hands in disbelief. 'I

19

mean, what the hell am I payin' him, five grand a month t' sit on his hands!'

Scarfe leaned toward him suddenly serious.

'Jim, nobody'll take him on. Not after what he did to those last couple o' guys.'

'Yeah, well ...' Beekman sighed. Managing the best bareknuckle fighter in Eastern America had seemed a good idea at the time. Jack Wilson was a brawling genius with a killer instinct, and he'd needed Beekman's underworld connections to follow his strictly illegal career. But without gloves or rules that killing instinct could get out of hand.

'Maybe we ought to set up a match between Wilson an' the rattler, huh?' Beekman laughed, his spirits reviving. He couldn't feel down on a day he'd made so much money.

'You'd lose a good rattler,' Scarfe grinned. He paused. 'Now there is a guy on the West Coast, named Philo Beddoe.'

'Philo Beddoe.' Beekman digested the name. 'I never heard of him.'

'Some folks in Dallas think a lot of him,' said Scarfe.

'Yeah?' In Beekman's book Texas ranchers and oilmen in white stetsons came close to Anthony Paoli. 'Which folks?' he asked.

'The folks that bet,' said Scarfe. 'An' he's well known in California. I think we could get a good piece of action on this one, Jim.'

Beekman considered it. At the moment Wilson was just a liability. Beekman didn't know the West Coast, but Patrick was sharp. He wouldn't mistake a good deal.

'All right.' Beekman nodded. 'You set it up.'

Satisfied, Scarfe smiled. 'All right,' he said and drained his glass.

Some three thousand miles due west and several hours later, Philo Beddoe burped contentedly and wondered, for at least the fifth time that day, at how swiftly his great decision had been made.

Beyond the windshield of his pick-up the blacktop

glistened under the headbeams. Orange groves filed past on either side. The night was balmy, moonless.

Decisions generally came easily to Philo. He'd learned to make them in the ring where time for cogitation was limited. If you chose right, you'd win; if not you'd probably end up on your back. There'd always be another time, another fight. Until now.

Could you change your life as easily as an opponent or a tactic? He sniffed, gripping the wheel.

All he knew was that he was at his peak now. The next move could only be down, and he had no intention of ending up one of those ageing, addle-brained stumble-bums who lived on hand-outs and tarnished memories.

No, he'd only look to the future now. He hiccuped gently. They'd celebrated his victory with a late lunch and rather too many Coors in a diner just outside Victorville - the name had appealed to Orville.

Now Philo was due to make the first important decision of the rest of his life.

He pulled over, braked and switched off the engine. Swinging down from the cab, he crossed the strip of stubby grass at the roadside and positioned himself in front of the nearest orange tree.

He reached down to his fly, unzipped and with a luxuriant sigh proceeded to hose the lower half of the trunk. Behind him Orville and Clyde stirred from a semi-doze, shook themselves and jumped after him.

A little over half a mile due east Luther Quince peered through the windshield of his Buick, his podgy fingers clamped over the top of the steering wheel. His small, piggy eyes shone excitedly out of the bloated folds of his face. He smacked his lips.

'Well, Loretta,' he said, 'we've talked about it for twenty years, but now, finally, we're doing it.'

He chuckled, unable to contain himself. He sucked breath into his mountainous, flabby body. 'We're in California!' he announced. Beside him - and only marginally less mountainous - his wife squinted anxiously at the dark road ahead. It had been just a week since Luther had retired on full pension from the Des Moines Power and Light company and they had been travelling ever since on a dream holiday which had been planned in detail. But for the first time Loretta Quince felt unease. 'I hear,' he confided to her husband, 'people here're a little peculiar.'

'Oh, Loretta!' Luther scoffed, shaking his head. That was Loretta all over. Full of fine words and high intentions and always backing down at the last moment. No wonder they'd never made this trip before. 'Folks're just folks the world over,' he told her, laughing.

It was at that moment the Buick's headbeams swept over the dark shape of a pick-up parked at the roadside. Besides it, in line, three figures were momentarily frozen in the glare; one tall, one medium-sized and one short and very hairy. Legs astride in an identical stance, all three were pissing earnestly into an orange grove.

A stunned silence fell over the car. They were nearly a mile down the road before Loretta Quince turned worried eyes on her husband.

'Luther,' she said.

'Yep?' he swallowed.

'I think we ought to go back t' Iowa.'

Country music thumped softly but unmistakably into the evening air as Philo swung the pick-up off a busy Lankershim Boulevard and passed beneath the neon sign that read: 'Palomino - Cocktails & Steaks'.

Easing into the parking lot, he braked and cut the engine. Orville and Clyde piled out of the cab after him.

A swift shower and a clean shirt at the Boggs homestead had refreshed Philo's body but there was still an uneasiness in his mind as he grabbed Clyde's hairy palm and strode towards the entrance to the bar. Orville seemed subdued too. Couldn't he just understand that Philo's life was changing? Philo stomped on the thought ruthlessly. Right now he needed sweet music, good company and a steady flow of ice cool beer. The rest of his life

22

could take care of itself.

Then Philo stepped inside and all thought of relaxation passed out of his head.

The Palomino Supper Club – premier country and western venue in the entire San Fernando Valley – was in lively, mid-week swing. Diners and drinkers mingled among the neat, dark-topped tables. Denimed urban cowboys, tee-shirted and stetsoned, drained beer from the bottle along the brass railed bar. A handful of couples waltzed western-style under the cluttered bandstand. Everywhere cigarette smoke curled and polished Fryes tapped out the rhythm of the local five-piece band and its guest singer.

The singer was all that gained Philo's attention. She was young and small, almost dwarfed by the heavy guitar she played. Long, platinum blonde hair swept to her shoulders, highlighted by the soft, lemon yellow dress she wore. She was not beautiful or conventionally pretty, but there was a luminous haunting quality about her face that clutched at Philo's heart.

Less than a year ago it had thrilled him in a way he hadn't known since adolescence. Tonight that same feeling stabbed at him like a knife.

'You didn't tell me she was here,' he snapped at Orville as they settled at the bar.

Orville's eyes widened in innocence. 'I didn't know. We c'n go.'

Philo ignored the suggestion. He ordered three beers, took a deep swig at his own and twisted on his stool to watch the performance.

Lynne Halsey-Taylor.

Last summer that slip of a girl had led him a dance that had ended abruptly in a Denver parking lot. With a masochistic relish, he recalled that parting scene – her shouts, her tears, her nails raking his flesh. Because he'd been fool enough to take her swiftly-offered love seriously, to return it with a depth of feeling, a trusting honesty she simply couldn't handle. Long suppressed bitterness welled up in him. His knuckles tightened round his beer.

23

Then how was it that just the sight of her could twist his stomach like that, set his fingers itching to clutch her warmth to him? It was like brawling with yourself. All you could get out of it was hurt.

Her song – it was a melodic ballad of a doomed affair – ended to loud applause.

'Lynne Halsey-Taylor, ladies and gentlemen!' announced the MC.

'Now let us have a big welcome for Johnny Duncan!'

As fresh applause rolled into the next set, Philo turned abruptly to the bar. Anger, curiosity and a perverse hope churned inside him. He lifted his beer.

'Mind if I sit here?'

She was already climbing onto the empty stool beside him. Her face loomed close, bright, questioning, serious.

Philo glanced away quickly. 'No, it's a free country.' He drank self-consciously, staring at the bottles behind the counter.

'You're still mad at me, I guess,' she said softly.

'No!' He swallowed. 'I like getting my guts kicked out.' Now he looked at her, eyes hard, fighting to keep the confusion of feelings out of his voice. She did not avoid his gaze.

'I didn't mean t' hurt you. I – ' And her courage faltered. 'I was ... mixed up.'

'Oh?' Philo said. 'Wha'do you think I was?'

A pink flush spread upwards from her neck. Her voice became almost a whisper. 'I'm sorry. But that's in the past.'

'Yeah.' Philo nodded. 'It sure is.'

Behind them the singer wailed of lost love and broken homes; it did little to fill their private silence.

'Do you want me to leave?' she said.

Philo sucked in breath, glanced from her to the bottle display. 'Yeah,' he said simply.

He did not look back until the bar stool was empty.

Sniffing, he turned to Clyde. The great ape blew him a wet and unmistakable raspberry.

Lynne Halsey-Taylor rounded the corner of the bar and

slipped onto an empty stool. Two stools away a tousle-haired cowboy in a bulging tee-shirt eyed her speculatively. Her glum gaze did not even acknowledge his existence. She was feeling very low. It had taken her long months to untangle her feelings about Philo, reconciling a lifetime of false hopes and inevitable disappointment with the trust and affection he'd offered so freely. Long, lonely nights – the loneliest spent with others – only confirmed what she'd suspected, and been terrified by, from the very beginning: she needed him. And now she'd stick around, take everything that was surely due to her, until Philo understood the decision she'd made.

Someone grunted beside her and a hairy form hauled itself onto the stool at her side. Clyde blinked solemnly at her, then picked up an empty beer can and banged it on the counter. Behind him the tousle-haired cowboy's eyes widened in disbelief.

'Awright, Clyde!' bellowed the bartender, hurrying over and guzzling the last of a hurried snack. 'Keep your pants on, I'm comin'.'

Lynne smiled gratefully at the great ape. In her short time with Philo she'd come to see Clyde as he did – as a distinct, if rather unconventional person.

She leaned her head close to his. 'I knew you and Philo came in here a lot, so I told 'em I'd sing for nothin', just to get a chance to talk to 'im,' she confided. 'Guess I shouldn't o' bothered, huh?'

The bartender cracked open a beer can and set it down in front of Clyde, whose horny fingers circled it immediately. He lifted the can and gulped at it. Behind him the cowboy's look of disbelief changed to disgust.

'I don't like drinkin' with filthy apes,' he announced to the bartender.

'Clyde,' the other replied, wiping a glass, 'is a clean ape.'

'Yeah?' Outraged, the cowboy rose from his stool. 'Well, I'm gonna kick 'is ass outa here.'

The bartender leaned forward confidentially. 'If I were you, friend, I'd just sit right back there and I'd have myself another beer.'

A sneer crossed the cowboy's face. He'd had a rough day and Lynne's blatant disregard of his charms had done nothing to improve it. 'You ain't me!' he snapped.

'Nope,' the bartender said affably.

Muscles tightening under his tee-shirt, the cowboy eased off his stool fixing a grim stare on the ape. Clyde continued to sup at his beer. His long right arm unhooked and draped itself casually over a brass railing that divided the bar counter at intervals. Without spilling a drop of drink, he gripped the metal in one hairy hand and bent it effortlessly through ninety degrees until it lay flat on the bar.

The cowboy turned quietly grey. Gently he eased himself back onto his stool.

'I'll have another beer,' he breathed.

'Right,' smiled the bartender.

From the farther end of the bar Philo had just glimpsed the conclusion of the incident.

'Looks like Clyde is getting a little rowdy,' he told Orville. He swallowed the last of his beer. 'We'd better get outta here.'

As Philo moved toward the exit, Orville moved down the bar to Clyde's stool and took a firm grip on his hand.

'You're gettin' rowdy, Clyde,' he told him quietly. The ape sniffed and shuffled onto the floor.

Orville found himself face to face with Lynne. His eyes darkened with suppressed anger. 'I want you t' leave Philo alone, honey,' he said.

'I'm not your honey,' she flared.

'Listen.' Orville bowed close. 'He was down for *two* months after you pushed 'im over.'

Lynne's annoyance died at this revelation.

'Well, so was I,' she said feebly.

'Well ...' Orville floundered momentarily in an emotional whirlpool that was already too complex for him. 'The three of us're doin' *fine* now,' he affirmed. 'So why do't ya just leave 'im alone.'

He nodded and backed away awkwardly, only to become aware that Clyde had slipped out of his hand. The ape suddenly appeared beside an alarmed cowboy, thrust his hairy jaws into the other's face and kissed him affectionately on the lips.

'Clyde, that's too much!' hissed Orville, grabbing for the orang-utan's hand. Immediately the ape swung around, aiming for a full bowl of fruit on a nearby table. 'Leave the bananas alone - c'mon!' rapped Orville. He hauled the unrepentant primate towards the exit.

A bemused cowboy turned to the bartender and sighed. 'Kind o' grows on ya, doesn't 'e?'

The bartender nodded and grinned.

Once the small, white-painted frame house in Pacoima had been modest but presentable, its narrow balcony overlooking a neat, well cropped suburban lawn. But that was long ago. As the neighbourhood had gently declined, so the house had decayed with it.

Now all that remained of the lawn was a sprinkling of sage and scrub that peeped fitfully between stacked tyres, gasoline cans, discarded bike frames and the dozen gleaming Harley-Davidson choppers parked in line across the entire frontage of the house. Similar mechanical debris cluttered the balcony and the white paint, now discoloured and flaking, was largely hidden by an array of signs, posters and placards, all bearing the scrawled image of a black widow spider.

As night threw a welcome darkness over this disordered scene, the throaty roar of a dozen masculine voices, shouting in unison, burst from within.

'We are the Black Widows.'

'Then who stomped a mud hole on ya?' bawled a solitary voice.

'Philo Beddoe!' came the instant response.

'Then spat on ya ... and let 'is ape stomp it dry?'

'Philo Beddoe!' the roar came again.

Charles Oliver Garfield Lapinsky - better known as Cholla - paused in mid-rant to survey his motley throng. Bare-armed and Levi-jacketed, they sprawled amongst the clutter of the living room - bike parts and TV sets, CBs

27

and highway signs – the looted debris of a life of petty crime. Cholla's heart swelled in pride, expanding the crudely tatooed black widow that clung to his beer gut.

God, those bikers looked mean. Mean enough to terrorise the entire San Fernando Valley, hard enough to wreak an awesome revenge on that diamond-knuckled dummy Beddoe who'd crossed them just once too often.

'So whose hide you gonna nail to the gates of hell?' Cholla bawled.

'Philo Beddoe!' the Black Widows bellowed, punching the air.

'All right then.' A savage grin cracked Cholla's ruddy, pock-marked visage. He slapped a riding crop into his fleshy palm.

'Let's start doin' some stompin' of our own!',

'Yeah!' 'Right!' Eyes agleam with blood-lust, the Widows rose as one – and froze as a plaintive cry went up from the rear.

'Good grief!' It came from a slight, thin-faced biker whose shoulder breadth could hardly contain the Widow emblem. 'My brownies are burnin'!'

'His what?' Cholla gaped in disbelief.

A musclebound bruiser blinked at him neanderthal-like from under a Nazi helmet decorated with steer horns.

'Elmo's baking brownies,' he explained.

Cholla's eyes grew round as Elmo bolted for the kitchen.

He raised them ceilingwards.

'Why me, Lord?' He spread his arms in supplication. 'I mean, you make other men outta clay. Mine – you make outta shit!'

CHAPTER 3

Philo backed a few inches along the dusty earth to avoid drips and squirted the silencer fitting with penetrating oil. Rust clung thickly there like some obscure growth and the silencer itself looked as if someone had peppered it with buckshot.

Knowing the dubious origin of some of Orville's wrecks, Philo reflected, it probably had been buckshot.

He rolled out from the beneath the ancient Chevy and stood up, blinking in the bright morning sunlight.

The car was parked some twenty feet short of the Boggs' homestead. It was a small single storey stucco and frame house tucked away at the end of a quiet residential block off Sunland Boulevard. Against its background of eucalyptus, scrub oak and Ma Boggs' own modest orange grove, it looked almost picturesque. But that was to ignore the half acre of wrecks and near wrecks that Orville's perfunctory repair business had amassed directly in front of it. Philo gazed across the automobile graveyard, looking for a Chevy of similar vintage. He might just be lucky enough to find an intact silencer.

He was only just realising he was out of luck when the porch door slammed and gravelly tones wafted through the air.

'Aaaah! Should've expected it!'

A small, scrawny figure, thin arms swinging, stomped off the porch and into the dust. For all her eighty years Ma Boggs moved with the restless vigour of an angry woman half her age.

'Expected what, Ma?' Philo asked mildly, glancing into the open bonnet.

'Quittin' your job!' his landlady growled. 'Lettin' an old lady die of frostbite and canker sores!'

Philo picked up an old screwdriver he had left on the air filter and moved back down the car.

'It ain't froze around here in thirty years, Ma,' he told her.

His landlady stamped flat heels on the ground. 'Don't have t' freeze. I got thin blood.'

'Besides,' added Philo, casting around for a spanner, 'I didn't quit my job. Fightin' ain't my job.'

'Yeah, well – ' Frustrated in her urge to have the argument she'd looked forward to, Ma glanced grumpily at her small flower garden. 'I have to admit it ain't much, but it's the closest you've come t' earnin' a decent livin'.'

Unmoved, Philo crouched and slid under the car.

Ma Boggs' face wrinkled in disgust. 'But hell!' she exploded. 'You don't care 'bout keepin' a roof over a poor helpless ol' lady's head. Ya don't care if she has to eat *dog* food!' She swung her arms wildly, relishing the outburst. 'Ya don't care if she has t' *soak* 'er teeth in Clorox!' She released her feelings in a loud and very wet raspberry that would have done Clyde credit – just as the great ape clattered through the porch door and loped round the side of the house. There was a half eaten packet of cookies in one hairy hand.

Ma gaped at him in outrage. She'd told Clyde a hundred times to stay away from her house – and especially her cookie jar. Good grief, he'd been eating in there and she hadn't even known.

'Come back here with my Oreos!' she bawled, lurching forward. 'Ya hairy ass!'

Under the car Philo chipped at the oil-softened rust and grinned. He was so involved he was not aware of anyone approaching until a male voice announced, 'I'm lookin' for Mister Philo Beddoe.'

Philo lifted his head and squinted at a pair of highly polished soft leather city shoes. The voice had smacked of the Bronx – in a tone that was used to swift responses. Instinctively it annoyed Philo.

'You're talkin' to 'im,' he said, scraping away the worst of the rust.

'I'm talkin' to 'is feet,' snapped the city shoes.

'Well – ' Philo reached for his spanner and tried it on

the silencer fitting; it was too small. 'The top half of 'im c'n hear ya,' he finished.

He noted that the shoes shuffled in annoyance. There was a soft sigh.

'I represent a man who would like to back you, Mr Beddoe.'

Philo tried the spanner a different way. Then he put it down.

'See that crescent wrench up on the top there?' he called.

There was a pause. 'Yeah, I see it.' The man sounded uneasy.

'Well, why don'tcha hand it to me,' suggested Philo. 'Tail first, of course, 'cause the jaws may be venomous.'

The sigh came again. The shoes spread and Philo glimpsed trouser bottoms of expensive mohair. A hand, cuffed in silk with heavy gold links, appeared and waved the grease-smeared wrench in Philo's general direction.

'Thanks,' he said, taking it and measuring it against the fitting.

He tightened it up. 'Back me in what?'

'A fight,' said city shoes simply.

'Sorry.' Philo took a firm grip on the wrench and pulled. 'I'm retired.'

'Since when?' snapped the other.

Philo pulled again, harder. It was no good; the whole assembly seemed to have corroded through. 'Since I, uh, decided t' retire,' he said.

He pulled again for luck, without result, and loosened the wrench.

City shoes seemed to take Philo's decision badly.

'My employer is willing to pay you *fifteen thousand* dollars for this fight, Mr Beddoe.' He paused as Philo slid out from beneath the car, wrench in hand, and rose beside him.

Involuntarily Patrick Scarfe stepped back a pace, his expression changing abruptly from peevish annoyance to nervous awe. Philo topped him by more than six inches; he seemed to be built like a cliff.

'Against who?' Philo asked.

Scarfe swallowed and recovered himself. If this man fought as well as he looked this could be the brawl of the century.

'A man named Jack Wilson. You know Wilson?' he enquired, fearing that the fighter's reputation could still ruin things. Philo appeared untroubled.

'I know of 'im,' he said.

Scarfe seized the chance. 'Let's not quibble, Mr Beddoe. *Twenty-five thousand*.'

Philo began to wipe his wrench with a rag he pulled from his pocket.

'Is that win or lose, or just win?' he asked

'The money will be payable – win *or* lose,' snapped Scarfe. Quickly he rifled his mohair jacket, retrieving a thick wad of bills and thrusting them under Philo's nose.

'Ten thousand in advance.'

Philo sniffed and looked away. 'Give it t' Clyde,' he said.

'Yes.' Scarfe glanced round swiftly. 'Who's Clyde?'

'He's my manager,' said Philo.

Scarfe nodded approvingly then jumped as a hand dropped amicably over his right shoulder. When he turned and found Clyde's simian visage less than three inches from his own, his alarm changed to a gasp of terror.

'Jes' Christ!'

'Don't worry,' Philo reassured him. 'He won't hurt ya.'

Scarfe's eyes became perfect circles. What kind of zoo was this place?

'You want me t' give ten thousand dollars – to an ape?'

Philo moved back towards the open bonnet. 'He handles all my business.' He nodded to the orang-utan.

'You stash that, Clyde – an' don't let Ma see ya.'

The great ape grunted and plucked the bills delicately from between Scarfe's nerveless fingers. The Easterner took a step backwards, extending a tentative hand to pat the orang-utan on the head.

'Good boy, good boy,' he murmured awkwardly. But Clyde was already loping and swinging his way round the back of the house. No one noticed a curtain shift in a front window and Ma Boggs' birdlike head dart in the direction the ape took.

'I - I'll be in touch,' said Scarfe, extracting a business card from his breast pocket and pushing it at Philo. Philo glanced at the card. It bore the name of James Beekman, and a New York telephone number. The name was familiar: a gambling bigshot with underworld connections.

'Yeah,' he said, bending over the bonnet. 'I'm sure.'

The night was warm and dark and clouds of incensed gnats were thrashing themselves against the insect screen on the Boggs porch.

Fifteen yards away Orville sprawled in the cab of his tow truck and debated whether to unleash some spray on them. So far it would mark the high point of the evening. With that Taylor woman appearing at the Palomino, Philo was showing an understandable reluctance to go near the place, and Orville had never liked solitary drinking. He had got so bored he had actually decided to work.

Behind the gentle murmur of Station KLAK - 'California Countree' - from a portable on the dashboard, the truck's CB rig buzzed and crackled. For long minutes Orville had been switching the dial from Triple A channels to private emergency repair services. It was his favourite - and most profitable - form of listening.

Then he struck gold.

'Ya there, Harry?' barked the speaker.

'Yeah,' came the reply. 'Wha'da ya got?'

Orville perked up. He recognised that voice.

'Dead battery at Sunset and Lincoln, Green seventy-three Chevrolet.'

There was a pause. 'Got it. Be about twenty minutes.' Orville gave an evil chuckle and began sorting through a thick file of placards jammed in the door pocket. 'Twenty minutes?' he murmured, grinning. 'It's too late by a half - Harry!'

He grunted in satisfaction and fished an oval plastic placard out of the sleeve. He glanced at it quickly. It read: 'HARRY'S 24-HOUR TOWING AUTO SERVICE'.

Then he leaned out the driver's window and slapped it in place on the door. 'Hang on, Green Chevy,' he cackled. 'Harry's on the way!' Bouncing across the seat, he slapped a second, identical placard on the passenger door.

He was twisting the ignition when Philo opened the insect screen and stepped out onto the porch.

'You seen Clyde?' he called.

Orville shook his head. 'No. Is 'e gone?'

Philo sighed and looked up and down the darkened junkyard.

'Been a couple o' hours.'

Orville nodded towards the back of the house.

'Is 'e in 'is shed?'

'I'll take another look,' said Philo.

Orville shrugged sympathetically, gunned the engine and swept off into the night to snatch fifteen dollars worth of business from the jaws of his unwitting competitor.

Clyde's shed was actually closer in size to a small barn. Constructed of boards, corrugated iron and other oddments from Orville's wreckyard, it stood across the yard at the back of the house – the furthest limit of the Boggs' domain. This was at Ma Boggs' strict insistence. Which made it all more surprising for Philo to hear her familiar grating tones issuing from within.

'No hairy ass jungle jumper is gonna outsmart Zenobia Boggs,' Philo heard as he cracked open the door. Under the glare of a naked light bulb, the old woman was crouching on the straw-strewn floor, rummaging through a battered cabin trunk which held Clyde's prized possessions. Philo grinned thinly. So she had overheard him with Beekman's hired hand.

'That goddam banana-head,' she growled, tossing half-unravelled sweaters and a thoroughly chewed football aside, 'probably ate it. Send 'im down to that . . .'

She became suddenly aware of Philo's presence, glanced at him and changed tack in mid-sentence: 'Work an' *slaaaave* for that ape o' yours. Work an' slaaaave . . .'

'Well I appreciate that, Ma,' said Philo. 'You haven't seen 'im, have ya?'

'No, no.' Ma made an unconvincing attempt to shuffle Clyde's assorted debris into neat piles. 'I ain't seen 'im,' she affirmed.

Behind her Philo turned and left, letting the door fall to. Ma Boggs immediately turned back to the trunk, rummaging even deeper and more vigorously than before. 'I'll find it,' she promised herself. 'You better *believe* I'll find it.'

Philo had cruised as far as the Tuxford turn-off before he finally acknowledged there could be only one place where Clyde was likely to be. The orang-utan wasn't normally a wanderer. If he waltzed off on his own it was generally for a specific reason at a specific destination.

He turned the pick-up right off Sunland Boulevard into Tuxford and accelerated to a steady fifty down the straight stretch that ducked under the Golden State Freeway. Reaching Lankershim, he swung left onto the broad carriageway. Presently he picked out the Palomino's signboard among the growing neon glitter on either side and signalled for the parking lot. As the engine died, Philo took a deep breath and let it out slowly.

It didn't stop the faint tingling about his heart, or the renewed sense of bitterness and injustice that seemed to swill about his gut.

Whatever he might consider the best course, fate seemed to be drawing him back to this place - and to her - just as the biggest offer of his professional career had appeared the day *after* his decision to retire. But accepting that had been a straightforward financial decision, hadn't it? For all her bitching, hadn't Ma Boggs been right about having enough money to live?

'Shee-it!' Philo smacked the dashboard in frustration. It was all getting too damn complicated. Snatching the keys, he swung out of the cab.

Tonight was a celebrity night at the Palomino, with Fats Domino's name up in lights, a higher cover charge and top prices at the bar. It also meant a packed floor and Philo had to squeeze his way to the drinks counter. A lilting guitar melody drifted above the murmur of conversation. Deliberately he did not look at the small, feminine figure singing on the bandstand.

Instead he beckoned to a familiar face behind the bar. 'You see Clyde?' he asked.

'Yeah.' The bartender nodded. 'Right behind ya, Philo.' Philo turned. Clyde was perched comfortably three tables from the front, watery eyes glued to the bandstand and with a can of beer grasped in one fist. The tables on either side were conspicuously empty.

Wincing, Philo threaded has way towards the ape and settled down next to him. Clyde turned and blew him a kiss.

On the bandstand Lynne Halsey-Taylor finished to modest applause, which Clyde joined in enthusiastically. As the compere thanked her, she smiled, her gaze flickering down shyly towards Philo. He returned her look awkwardly, his throat catching. She looked about twelve years old. She stepped down onto the floor as the star turn was announced behind her. To cheers and loud applause Fats Domino rolled on stage, bowed and sat down at the piano, immediately pounding into his first number.

Lynne settled at Philo's table, her eyes still watching him warily.

Philo nodded at Clyde. 'He ain't supposed t' be out like this,' he said. His unease made the remark come out more harshly than he'd intended.

'Wha' did I do?' Lynne reacted. 'I was just singin' a number an' he came in an' sat down.'

Philo looked away. He didn't want to argue. 'Probably got lost an' recognised this place - ' he offered.

'Maybe he wanted t' see me.' Lynne's eyes dropped to the table top. 'Not everybody hates me, you know.'

'I don't hate ya,' said Philo, rapping his knuckles on the table and wishing he had a drink to hold. 'Oh, I c'n take just about any kind of pain. There's just one I - have no tolerance for.'

Lynne's gaze sought his. 'Some kinds I can't tolerate either,' she said quietly.

Philo let the breath ease out of his lungs. However bruised, however resentful he felt, something electric still flowed between them.

'Ya gonna do another set?' he asked.

She shook her head, blonde hair swirling.

'No, I'm just doing one set a night. They're all here t' see Fats.'

Philo's gaze steadied on her. 'You sound good.'

She nodded. 'Thank you.'

'Real good,' Philo told her. On stage Fats' song swelled into a chorus, drowning them both out. Philo waited patiently.

'Do you have any wheels?' he asked at last.

Lynne looked down at the table. 'Nope,' she said softly.

'Give you a ride home,' Philo said. 'If you like.'

Lynne glanced up at him. 'I like.'

'Yeah,' murmured Philo, rising and taking Clyde's hand. He was silent as the Apache pulled out onto Lankershim and headed north at Lynne's direction, but his mind was a ferment of doubt and troubled memories. It had been just such a night when he'd first met Lynne and whisked her home to a trailer park to find – what had been the boyfriend's name? Schuster? Schyler? A petulant blond youth whose weakness and dependence had shackled her more securely than a houseful of kids and a drunken husband. A simpering prop to Lynne's own lack of self esteem. In the long months since, Philo had come to realise that – though without properly understanding or excusing it. It was hard to despise the person you loved, harder still to walk willingly into the same trap – however contrite the bait might appear. His heart was thudding as he turned off the main drag on the outskirts of San Fernando, pulled into a quiet tree-lined residential street and halted. To his surprise he found himself opposite the local YWCA.

He blinked at Lynne. 'This is it?'

She tossed her head. 'Anything wrong with it?'

Her gaze held him, daring him to ask the dozens of self-revealing questions that danced in his stare. But he only

37

said, 'No, not a thing.'

She softened, her hand reaching to the door handle. 'Well, I guess I can't ask you in.'

'I guess not,' said Philo.

She clicked open the door, climbed down and crossed the road. Beneath the dim light that overhung the hostel's entrance, she turned and waved.

'Bye Clyde. Thanks Philo.'

In that brief instant she looked waiflike and lost to Philo, more lonely than he had ever seen anybody before. Then Clyde was gibbering goodbye, his lips smacking affectionately and Philo found himself nodding curtly, too confused in his emotions to betray anything, as he let go the brake and moved off swiftly into the night. In silence he found the main drag again, waited for lights then turned right, back towards L.A. It was late now and traffic was light. The pavements were empty, glistening in the glare of unheeded store windows. For all the heat of the day still oozing up from the tarmac and the paving stones, the night seemed suddenly cold to Philo – cold and a little bleak.

He glanced at Clyde. The ape's ponderous eyebrows were low, his eyes wandering reproachfully beneath them. His long arms dangled in front of him. He was sulking.

'Shut up, meathead,' Philo growled. Criticism from an ape – buddy or not – was something he could do without right now. He upped his speed a fraction, concentrating on the road ahead. Concentrating so hard he quite failed to notice the line of Harley choppers strung across the side street, the black widow decal gleaming darkly on each burnished fuel tank.

'Hey!' cried a joyful Cholla as a dozen bikers turned as one. 'It's Philo Beddoe!'

Grins of obscene delight flashed from Widow to Widow. A dull evening was beginning to look up.

Cholla wrenched at his throttle grip, his engine screaming. 'Are we bad mothers?' he bellowed above the roar.

'We are bad mothers!' the massed Widows replied.

And with squealing tyres they rocketed off in hot pursuit.

CHAPTER 4

Up ahead a stop light flickered to red and Philo, still wrapped in thought, braked and pulled to a halt. He was only dimly aware of the full roar of motorcycles at his rear, until a gleeful and familiar voice called out:

'Hey Beddoe – it's us!'

Philo turned his head. The entire Black Widow gang were strung out across the width of the road to his right – in a long and intimidating line. At least they would have been intimidating, Philo considered, if they had not consisted of the stupidest, greasiest, most slack-jawed sons of bitches this side of Alaska. He sighed, recalling a series of farcical incidents the previous summer during which he had single-handedly and with minimal effort disposed of most of the Black Widow bike fleet.

'You talkin' to me?' he drawled, turning back to the road ahead. On past history he was in more danger from a berserk motorist jumping the lights than from Cholla and his sidekicks.

Cholla gave a low throaty chuckle, his pot belly quivering in time to it. 'I ain't talkin' t' you, Beddoe,' he snarled. 'I'm readin' your death warrant!'

Philo stared through the windshield. 'I didn't know you boys could read.'

A sneer split Cholla's grimy, pitted visage. The overweight biker leaned close to the pick-up's passenger window.

'Oh, now that's real cute. Real cute,' he mouthed. 'We're gonna kill you slow, boy. Take maybe a week!'

Philo blinked slowly. 'Well, I wouldn't wanna rush you,' he commented.

'Yeah.' Cholla straightened, enjoying himself immensely.

'After the first day, I think, you're probably gonna be *shakin'* – like some blind faggot at a weenie roast!' He exploded into raucous guffaws, which the grinning, eager-eyed Widows took up on cue.

Elmo, the weediest, aimed a friendly nudge at Cholla's elbow. 'You got 'im real good, Cholla,' he cried. 'You got 'im real good with that one.'

'Shut your hole!' Cholla's expression froze momentarily. It softened as he turned back to Philo. ''Cept, uh, this time,' he continued, 'ain't gonna be no weenie roast.' Fresh guffaws overtook him. 'No, this time it's gonna be a ... *ape roast*!'

Gales of laughter swept up and down the line of bikers. In the pick-up Philo's face became stone-like. Taunts from the Widows were so much hot air as far as he was concerned, but threatening a friend of his – and especially Clyde – was something else.

The lights changed to green. Philo eased off the hand brake. 'Right turn, Clyde,' he ordered.

With a speed born of long practice, Clyde's long hairy forearm shot from the passenger window. Its bunched fist connected neatly with Cholla's jaw. Groaning, the biker tumbled sideways, his machine crashing into Elmo's which struck Dallas's which struck Frank's, and the whole line went down in a protesting mass like a pack of cards.

Without a backward glance, Philo drove smoothly across the intersection and off into the night.

'Hey, Cholla,' cried Elmo, pinned beneath his leader's bulk. 'They're gettin' away!'

Still inclined at a forty-five degree angle, Cholla sighed, his eyes rolling sideways towards the stars.

'Why me?' he begged softly.

Two miles down the road, Philo also sighed. As usual, action, however slight, had cleared his head.

He turned to Clyde, 'Ah, what the hell ... I guess maybe it's time.'

And he swung the pick-up in a tight circle.

Five minutes later he was standing in the entrance hall of the local YWCA, leaning anxiously across the reception desk while a prim desk clerk checked her signing-in book. Behind him two inmates hovered by a notice board, throwing him curious and admiring glances.

'She's in room twenty-five,' the clerk said at last. 'But you can't go up there.'

'No, ma'am,' Philo nodded. 'I know that.'

He moved quickly round the two inmates and vaulted up the stairs. Open-mouthed the girls looked back at the desk clerk, who was snatching up the telephone. 'Operator,' she cried, 'get me the police!'

Philo paused at the first floor landing. A wall notice next to a fire door announced room numbers one to thirty-five. Feminine chatter floated up the stairwell. He pushed through the door into a narrow corridor with room number one on his right. Two or three girls turned and gaped at him. They were in dressing gowns or slips. The nearest did not notice him until he squeezed past her, nodding politely.

'Oh, uh, 'scuse me, ma'am.'

Her jaw dropped as he moved purposefully down the corridor. With a shriek one of the dressing gowned girls backed swiftly into her room.

A door snapped open on his left and a short, buxom redhead stepped into him, steam billowing behind her. Seeing him, she blinked and jumped, the narrow bath towel wrapped round her body slipping down her pronounced cleavage.

'Hey!' she called, recovering herself and tightening the towel.

'Wait a minute!'

'Excuse me, ma'am!' Philo tossed over his shoulder. 'I didn't see a thing. Hardly.'

'You aren't allowed up here!' the redhead yelled.

'I know that, ma'am,' Philo agreed.

He was opposite room twenty-five. As the queries and protests rose in volume behind him, he knocked on the door.

'Who is it?' came Lynne's voice from inside.

'Philo,' he called.

The door cracked open. Lynne peeped wide-eyed round the edge. She was still in her outdoor clothes.

41

'You're not allowed up here,' she said incredulously.

Philo glanced down the corridor and gave a wry smile. 'Well, it must be true, you're the third person who's told me that.'

He pushed past her, closing the door, and hovered, his decisiveness of the past few minutes drooping somewhat. Lynne moved uncertainly towards the bed. She sat down and shrugged.

'Well ...'

Philo straightened. 'Well,' he finished for her, 'we've got an extra room at the house.'

Lynne's gaze hardened moodily. 'I don't need any handouts,' she told him.

'Handouts're what you get from the government,' Philo snapped. 'A hand-up is what you get from friends.'

She looked at him, searching his face. Then she said quietly, 'Are you a friend?'.

Philo didn't hesitate. 'I'm a friend.'

And no more? Lynne asked herself. Outside a police siren wailed, postponing an immediate answer. Lynne sprang to her feet.

'Well, I don't have so many friends that I c't afford t' lose one,' she grinned awkwardly.

The two young patrolmen took the stairs at a sprint, then were forced to a polite shuffle as they entered the crowded first floor corridor. As news of their arrival spread, the inmates squeezed back on either side.

'Down there,' they were told. 'Number twenty-five.'

'He's big.' Someone giggled.

Nodding, the policemen paused outside Lynne's door and drew night sticks. The corridor quieted as the taller of the two knocked. Inside Lynne cleared her throat, as though newly woken.

'What is it?' she called.

The shorter, bespectacled officer opened the door. It was dark inside. The corridor light spilled across the bedsheet and showed Lynne's head, poking above the top of it. Her hair was mussed and she blinked, bleary-eyed.

'Sorry, ma'am,' said the officer. Glancing at his

42

companion, he closed the door again.

The moment he had gone Lynne sprang out of bed and dragged a suitcase up off the floor. Philo rolled out from under the bed, went to the window and yanked it up. While Lynne stuffed toiletries into her suitcase, Philo inspected the fire escape outside. In seconds they were both tip-toeing down the newly painted ironwork. Inside, the corridor was buzzing with disbelief and protest.

'I think what we got here, ladies,' interrupted the tall officer, raising his arm, 'is a case of wishful thinkin'.'

Exasperation flashed across half a dozen faces. The buxom redhead, still clad precariously in her towel, fanned her lashes furiously at a lanky brunette who loomed beside her, toothbrush in hand and her thin lips smeared with foam.

'They all think we moon around all day, lustin' after their bodies,' she cooed in mock Southern drawl.

'Well, some of us do, Rita!' mouthed the brunette, and instantly crushed the tall officer to her bosom, planting a wet and foaming kiss squarely on his mouth. Shrieks of laughter pierced the air. Shaken to the core, the policeman reeled back, spitting toothpaste. Outside, Philo and Lynne stepped down lightly into a flowerbed, glanced up at the building and crossed a narrow lawn to the roadway. Philo's pick-up was at the kerb - barely ten yards behind the police car. Philo eased open the passenger door, tucked Lynne's suitcase inside, then helped her up. A frown crossed his forehead.

'Where's Clyde?' He glanced round. A familiar outline bobbed into view in the front seat of the patrol car. Philo sucked in breath. 'Oh shit!'

He hared along the pavement, jerked open the driver's door and snatched Clyde's paw just as the orang-utan finished the business at hand, gibbering contentedly. The bespectacled officer was laughing as he followed his grim-faced companion out of the hostel entrance. He couldn't wait to get back to the station with this one.

'Ah well.' He slipped his nightstick back into its holster. 'So how ya gonna write this one off?'

'I'm not,' his companion muttered. 'Plus, you were a lot o' help.'

'Well,' the other grinned, 'you could always say she was nuts about your toothpaste smile.'

He burst into renewed laughter as they rounded the corner of the building and approached their car.

'Or,' the bespectacled officer went on, relishing the moment, 'you could bust 'em for harassin' an officer.'

'Just shut up!' the tall one snarled. He reached for the driver's door, just as his companion let out a yell.

'Hey!' He was pointing at a battered pick-up retreating slowly up the street away from them. Philo and Lynne were plainly visible behind the wheel. 'It's them!' shouted the bespectacled officer.

With a squeal of tyres, the pick-up lurched across the street, turned and shot up a side turning.

Flinging open the car doors, both officers jumped inside.

'C'mon! C'mon!' the bespectacled one urged. 'We c'n catch 'em!'

To his surprise the tall patrolman was staring down in horror at his lap. Spread by his descending rear, a brown stickiness was oozing over the edge of the seat. 'You catch 'em!' he roared. Then the stench hit them both.

Friends, thought Lynne, wriggling her toes in Philo's bed.

'Does that mean "no-hard-feelings-but-keep-your-distance" friends? Or "lower-your-guard-then-I'll-show-you-what-hurting-means" friends?'

She bit her lip deliberately, forcing herself not to think negatively. This time, however it turned out, it wasn't going to be her own sour feelings that made it go wrong.

She looked down the bed, finding it odd that this was the first occasion she had actually climbed into it. It seemed ridiculously small for a man of Philo's size – a narrow, metal frame single bed, hardly bigger than a sleeping bag. The room itself wasn't that much larger: just enough room for a dresser, a chair and a tiny sink. The decorations were minimal: a faded sports poster in a corner, an out of date calendar beside a mirror above the sink.

Lynne felt a touch of sadness. Her room in the Y had been homelier than this.

There was a knock on the door. After a pause Philo poked his head round, saw that Lynne was tucked in and nodded.

'So – where're you gonna sleep?' Lynne asked.

Philo grunted. 'We have a – guest room out back. I told ya.'

He grunted again. 'Goodnight.'

'Goodnight.' Lynne spoke softly to a closing door. She head his footsteps across the hall, then the clicking of a side door. Throwing back the sheet, she bounced across to the window and pulled the curtain back carefully.

Philo was crossing the yard outside, making for a small barn on the further side. There was a sleeping bag rolled under his arm.

Lynne's full lips curled into a smile. She watched Philo unlock the barn door and enter, a dim light flickering on inside. After a moment she let the curtain fall back. Her smile broadened. Then she hopped off the bed and made for the door.

'Well Clyde – you still up?' Philo asked, unrolling his sleeping bag across the straw.

Clyde blinked at him and gibbered quietly from the far end of the shed. He was perched on a tattered armchair with horsehair bursting from its arms.

Making a cooing sound, he advanced on Philo.

'Wha'da ya doin' now?' said Philo, turning to him.

The great ape produced a thin disc from his clenched fist and pressed it into Philo's hand.

Philo grinned. 'An Oreo cookie for me? I'll save mine for later,' he promised, slipping it under his sleeping bag. Content, Clyde leaned forward and smacked Philo affectionately on the lips.

'Ol' buddy.' Philo shrugged off his shirt, boots and

45

jeans and padded across the the door to switch out the light. When he got back to his sleeping bag, the orang-utan was curled on the further side. Philo crawled in beside him and turned over to sleep. A hairy forearm draped comfortingly over his shoulder.

He had hardly closed his eyes when the shed door creaked open. Sitting up, he saw Lynne poised wary and bright-eyed in the doorway. She was wearing a knee-length white night shift and her feet were bare. 'Mind if I come in?' she asked.

'No.' Philo blinked at her. 'Not at all.'

Grinning, she moved over to him, kneeling on the sleeping bag. There was a soft crunch.

'What was that?' she said.

Philo glanced at Clyde. 'Just a cookie I was savin' till later.' He brushed the crumbs away, and Lynne shuffled closer to him.

'Well, never mind,' she whispered, gazing straight into his eyes. 'You c'n have me instead.'

A smile spread across Philo's face. He turned to Clyde. 'No lookin' now,' he warned.

He pressed his lips to Lynne's as she moulded herself against him.

Clyde surfaced from sleep in a bright bar of sunlight. There were several all about the sleeping threesome, shafting through cracks in the shed walls and churning dust motes in the clear, still air.

Rolling away from Philo, the great ape planted a kiss on Lynne's cheek. Whistling, he shuffled to the opposite end of the shed and paused beneath a scrap of newspaper pinned to the wall. It showed a photograph of a female orang-utan called Bonnie which had just been acquired by Bakersfield Zoo; Philo had saved the cutting from the previous day's paper. Clyde hooted softly and smacked a kiss against the crumpled paper. Then, with a louder hoot, he scampered across the shed and out of the door. Roused by the sound, Philo stirred, feeling the companionable warmth of Lynne's body against him. He sat up.

It had been so good. Far better than he'd remembered.

And not just good sex. That wasn't so hard to find. This was something beyond that, something that made every stroke, every caress, every touch precious, a joyous rediscovery of a truth he'd known inside himself for ages and somehow, stupidly forgotten. Lynne moved beside him. She opened her eyes and smiled. Then she raised her head, turning it to one side to look for Clyde. 'Oooh,' she murmured. 'We chased 'im away.'

Philo smiled down at her. 'Fresh air is good for 'im,' he said. 'Besides he'll guard the door.'

Lynne raised her eyebrows. 'Is he reliable?'

'Anything that gets past Clyde,' Philo assured her, 'is forty feet high with fangs.'

Lynne laughed and lowered her head back on the sleeping bag. 'I think we're safe.'

'I think,' nodded Philo.

Lynne breathed out, her eyes fastening on Philo; they were soft and warm.

'I think I love you,' she said quietly.

Philo sighed gently, savouring the warmth of her gaze. 'I think that's a piece of luck for me,' he concluded and bent to kiss her.

Clyde shambled about the automobile junkyard, examining lengths of rusted fender for grubs, rolling battered hub caps experimentally along the ground and then taking a few practice swings on an old rubber tyre Philo had strung up for him from the limb of a scrawny eucalyptus.

He was mildly bored. Philo had fed him a plateful of oats and bananas before driving Lynne back to San Fernando and the ape had looked forward to a friendly wrestle or a diverting game of tag on his friend's return. But instead Philo had dived straight into the house.

Cracking a particularly large flea between thumb and forefinger, Clyde looked up at the porch. He whistled and cooed happily. Philo had reappeared in a light grey tracksuit and training shoes.

As the ape jumped down from the swing and bowled towards him, Orville's tow truck swung in off the dirt road in a cloud of dust. A large red Mercedes saloon hung behind it.

Orville braked as he drew level with Clyde and stuck his head out the cab window.

'Philo!' he called. 'Jordan said he'd give us two hundred big ones if we'd scrap that Merc for 'im.' He jerked his thumb backwards.

Philo nodded, stepping down off the porch. 'Great. Clyde!'

The orang-utan's head swivelled round, eyes glistening. 'Scrap the Merc.'

Inside the cab, Orville stabbed the hoist button. The motor whirred and the vehicle behind him settled slowly onto the ground.

'C'mon, Clyde,' he called, climbing out the cab and unhitching the tow hook. 'Ya got work t' do!'

The great ape gibbered happily, Philo forgotten. Bounding past Orville, he landed on the saloon's roof with a force that buckled it several inches inward. A door clicked open. Reaching down, Clyde began to yank at it.

Orville bundled the tow hook in the back of his truck and moved toward the cab to park the vehicle closer to the house. As he opened the door, the Merc's door flew past him. He looked back in alarm – to catch the saloon's driving seat rocketing out the gap where the door had been. Inside the car Clyde was hooting and whistling, bouncing up and down on the front passenger seat which came loose with a sudden crack, tumbling him backwards and out of sight. Seconds later that seat too skidded across the dirt.

Orville swallowed and looked round uneasily for Philo. As a breaker of old automobiles Clyde in full destructive spate was an undeniable asset. If only he could be absolutely certain the ape would stop with the car …

Orville climbed into the cab and through the passenger window glimpsed Philo jogging easily along the road in the direction of Sunland. Sighing, he lifted the handbrake and moved away. As he went, the Merc's front passenger door cartwheeled past him on the right and thudded into Ma Boggs' flower patch.

Orville winced and began to swear silently.

CHAPTER 5

It was still early when Philo reached the highway but the sun was already beginning to scald. His training shoes kicked dust behind him and there was a whiff of exhaust in the air.

He paused on the hard shoulder then turned away from the clutter of gas stations and car washes, the small factories and the odd isolated house that marked this edge of civilisation.

He started down the highway toward the hills, breathing steadily and easily, relishing the power in his leg muscles as the sweat began to ooze from his pores.

He felt good, very good. This morning's jog would be no effort at all. After last night he could throw in a tour of the San Gabriels that loomed to the east and not miss a breath.

He was so engrossed in his own state of mind that he barely noticed the tall man in the blue tracksuit who was tying his shoelace at the roadside. As Philo passed, the tall man's eyes followed him. After a few seconds he sprang to his feet and trotted in Philo's wake.

'Mind if I join you?' he panted, drawing level.

Philo glanced at him in mild surprise. Joggers weren't normally so sociable. The newcomer was Philo's height too, and at least as broad.

'Hell, no.'

The tall man nodded companionably and matched strides. He had a wide, handsome face, dark hair and a narrow, bushy moustache. For all its affability it seemed a face that would brook little nonsense if the mood took it. And, Philo decided, they could both be the same age – or close enough to make no difference.

They jogged on in silence. An occasional car or truck swished by. The highway was mostly quiet.

'We must be three miles out,' the newcomer panted.

'How much further 'fore you turn back?'

'About a couple more,' said Philo.

The newcomer shook his head admiringly.

'That's ten miles round trip. You do this every day?'

Philo shrugged. 'More or less.'

The other man laughed. 'Well I'm not sure I'm gonna make it. I'm kind o' new to this physical stuff.'

Philo glanced at him oddly. For all his protestation there was no more than a thin film of sweat on the man's forehead. And he hadn't yielded an inch to Philo since he'd begun jogging.

'Well – ' Philo gave him a wry smile. 'You're doin' real good.'

'Well thanks.' The newcomer took the compliment straight. 'The doc said I had t' get some exercise. All I do is sit behind a desk all day.'

Philo peeled off the hard shoulder and down onto a dirt track.

'You *sit* behind it or you carry it round?' he called behind him.

The other man laughed and followed him. 'Well,' he conceded. 'I play a little squash sometimes.'

The track broadened into a wide, wheel-rutted expanse between empty corrugated sheds and abandoned derricks; cables and rusting machine parts peeped through the dust. It was an old open cast mine, chewed out of the foothills of the San Gabriels. The workers had moved on years before. Philo vaulted a low shute that had once held sluice water and padded onto a worn, scrub-grown pathway beyond. The newcomer matched his jump without difficulty, then blinked suddenly at the view beyond.

There was blue sky and great deal of empty air. It was the furthest limit of the workings, a man-made cliff that dropped cleanly three hundred, four hundred feet, though wind and heat had eroded the very top and the pathway that wound along it, leaving deep, unexpected crevices and channels.

Philo jumped a three-foot crack without a second

glance. More wary, the tall man let him take the lead.

'You look like you do some liftin',' he called.

'Yeah, a little.' Philo sniffed. 'Mostly engine blocks.'

The other raised his eyebrows.

'That'll do the job – '

'Careful of that soft shoulder there,' Philo interrupted him, skipping sideways. A big bite had been taken out of the cliff where a crescent-shaped section thirty to forty feet long had collapsed, leaving a small knoll at either end. The newcomer rounded the nearest knoll, staring down at the cliff edge. The bite looked like it had been cut with a razor. It was obviously quite recent.

'It's a hell of a drop,' he commented.

Philo nodded as he rounded the second knoll. Behind him came a low rumble. He spun in time to see the tall man balancing on the edge of the precipice on one leg, his arms flailing. Then, in a billow of dust he had gone.

Swearing, Philo turned quickly, flattening himself against the dry crumbling earth. Another bite, only three or four feet wide, had eaten into the cliff path. He squirmed to the edge, hearing the dislodged earth echo and boom down the cliffside.

Three feet below him, his face set in a mask of pain and controlled panic, the tall man clung to a length of ancient cable by a single hand. He was breathing explosively, swinging his legs over emptiness in an effort to bring up his other arm. As it rose, Philo threw his arm down, grasping the other's hand, wrist to wrist. For a moment the newcomer hung crabwise against the cliffside. Then, sucking in deep breaths, Philo took the strain. The man was heavy, a good two hundred pounds, and his attempts to lighten Philo's load by clawing his way up the cable with his free hand made only a marginal difference. By the time he sprawled safely on the cliff top, both men were gasping and groaning.

'Hey.' Philo grinned at him between breaths. 'You got a pretty good grip for a new guy.'

The other man's head was still down. 'There's a lot o' strength in fear.' He shook himself and sat up, looking straight at Philo. 'I believe I owe ya.'

Philo nodded, and climbed to his feet. 'I believe you do,' he said.

He twisted his wrist, urging the circulation to reflow. Then he turned and began jogging along the path again. In a moment the tall man struggled to his feet and followed him.

Gnats divebombed the porch light as Orville slumped beneath it in the cool of the evening. He had come home late after snatching probably the worst taco that had ever curled up and died on a roadside stand, and he was feeling peeved. Peeved with himself for making an awful buy, but even more peeved with Philo who seemed to have incarcerated himself in his room, from which emerged sounds of teeth-brushing, washing and general titivation.

Orville sniffed, sinking deeper into his ragged wicker chair.

He cracked a pistachio between his teeth, extracted the nut and passed it across a small table to Clyde who was perched on an adjacent bench.

Behind them a door opened in the house and Philo's heavy tread sounded in the hallway. He pushed through the insect screen, looking spruce in newly pressed jeans and a fresh tee-shirt. Instantly Orville was rocketing forward, his clown's face set in an expression of dire seriousness.

'Philo!' he snapped. 'You can't do this fight.'

Philo looked at him and frowned.

'Why not?' he asked.

'Well – ' Orville's gaze wavered; it had never been their style to criticise each other and he didn't like to start now.

'I've been checkin' with some people an' I found out who Jack Wilson is.'

To his dismay Philo seemed less than pleased.

'Look,' he said, 'the fight's gonna get us a new truck, maybe a new roof an' a few extras for Ma.'

'He killed two men last year!' Orville snapped.

'One,' said Philo dully.

'So what? The other one's lyin' someplace with

52

nothin' below the neck but memories!'

Philo put his hand against a support post and looked out in the darkness. 'Well, I told 'em I was gonna do it,' he said.

This reasonableness seemed more like the old Philo. Orville became more placatory.

'I know I don't have much influence with ya any more, since ya got a girlfriend' - his head danced about mournfully, 'but *damn it*, Philo, ya can't do this!'

Philo straightened. 'Well, I'm gonna do it.' His eyes flickered at Orville, then hardened in warning. 'Don't you go tellin' Lynne about Wilson now, ya hear?' And he strode off the porch towards his pick-up.

'Damn!' Orville swore under his breath and kicked at a porch post. Once he'd been able to talk to Philo, now he seemed to put his foot in it every time he opened his mouth.

The pick-up started up and purred away towards town.

Orville winced and looked across at Clyde who looked back with sad, watery eyes.

'Yeah, Clyde,' Orville nodded. 'Looks like both of us 're gettin' aced.' He stared into the night. 'Yeah ...'

Tonight was Friday, payday for many in the San Fernando Valley, and the Palomino was getting much of the benefit. It was hot and crowded with all tables occupied, the conversation raucous and the smoke fug thick in the air.

After a brief drink with Lynne, Philo settled on a stool at the end of the bar to watch her set. Tonight, dressed in a pale, clinging dress, she looked radiant. Her songs might be of adultery and doom but her eyes - especially when they met Philo's - blazed the opposite.

Halfway through the last, someone murmured, 'Mind if I sit?' and moved onto the stool behind Philo. He nodded, throwing them a half glance. Then he looked properly. It was the jogger from this morning, smartly dressed now in a dark suit and tie that quite failed to disguise his physique.

'Okay,' Philo smiled in greeting. This was a little too

much of a coincidence. The man seemed an unlikely country and western fan.

The jogger sipped at his drink – a soft drink, Philo noticed.

He nodded at Lynne.

'Friend of yours?'

'Yeah.' Philo's satisfaction and pride was plain.

'Nice voice,' the other noted. 'Nice style.' The two men swapped appreciative smiles.

'I think so,' Philo agreed.

Lynne's song faded to a close amid loud applause and cheers. It was a warm and responsive crowd – but at least one member was inclined to overstep the limit. As Lynne bowed and beamed in gratitude, a burly man in check shirt and stetson rose from a table directly in front of Philo.

'Why don't cha get somebody who c'n sing around here!' he bawled, his heavy face flushed with drink. Three similarly soused companions at his table burst into loud laughter.

Lynne stepped off the bandstand and threaded her way to Philo, ignoring the comments. She smiled at him and climbed on a stool next to him.

The burly drunk followed her with his eyes, swaying gently on his feet.

Philo turned to order Lynne a drink.

'Uhhhh – that's not polite,' he heard. It was the jogger. That affable look had gone. His eyes were sharp and cold, focused on the swaying drunk.

'Ah, forget it,' said Philo.

But the challenge had already been accepted.

A broad grin spread on the drunk's face. His eyes gleamed and his massive shoulders hunched.

'The complaint department's open now, sonny!' he boomed.

The jogger skipped off his stool, straight into a swinging right that snapped his head round and sent him tumbling to the floor.

Philo reacted immediately.

Leaping forward, he slammed two sharp jabs into the drunk's bulging gut before he had recovered from his swing. As the burly man doubled in pain, Philo punched hard at his kidney. Gasping, the drunk reeled backwards across his table, overturning it and making his three companions spring up from their chairs in protest and alarm. Then all three flew at Philo.

Two tried to grab his arms. Philo floored the one on the right with an elbow in the stomach and a swift left jab. Ducking a swing from the man on the left, he brought his knee up into the fellow's crotch, swinging a right at his head. As it connected, the third attacker unleashed a series of hammer blows at Philo's chest and stomach.

Winded, Philo fell back, absorbing the pain of the attack, waiting for the right opening. Dimly he was aware of the band on stage pounding away manfully above the sounds of destruction.

Then he saw his chance. His right fist shot out, catching his attacker under the heart. The man gasped, groaned as Philo followed up with cracking blows to his head and jaw. As the dismayed attacker lurched backwards, Philo blocked a swing from the man on the left and turned on him.

Rising from the floor, the tall jogger watched with interest. This quarrelsome quartet were big men, seasoned brawlers who could jointly make mincemeat of any other man in the room. But Philo wasn't just holding his own, he was hurting them. Then behind the central action the burly drunk found his feet again. Kicking aside the table, he stumbled towards Philo's back, his eyes dark with venom. And the jogger saw the switchblade in his hand.

He came up like spring steel, one fist snapping the blade from the drunk's hand while the other pounded into his jaw. Two more rapid jabs sent the astonished drunk back onto the floor. Then he had turned onto the three still occupying Philo. Two hammer blows, to the left and right, and Philo realised he was redundant.

Wiping a trickle of blood from his mouth, he stumbled back against the bar, squeezing Lynne's hand. Then he watched the jogger finish the fight.

It was a clean, sharp, utterly ruthless performance; it had the economy, the pride in effort, the deadliness of a professional.

As it ended, with two men unconscious and the third nursing what appeared to be a broken jaw, Philo had no doubt as to the identity of his saviour.

Taking a deep, satisfied breath, the jogger straightened his suit, smoothed his hair and rejoined Philo at the bar.

'You play a hell of a game of squash,' said Philo. The other blinked and nodded. 'So do you.' He picked up his drink and touched it against Philo's. 'Believe that makes us even,' he said.

'I believe it does,' Philo agreed. He kept his eyes on the other. 'Did you find out what you wanna know?'

Jack Wilson hesitated before answering. He hadn't meant to be so obvious, but then he'd very rarely fought a man of Philo's reputation or – to judge by his recent performance – Philo's calibre.

He allowed himself a wry smile. 'Yeah, I did.' He glanced down at his drink. 'You're fast an' you like pain. Ya eat it like candy.' He lifted his head. 'Oh, I seen a few cases like that in my time. Ya know, the more they get hurt, the more dangerous they become. But ya gotta be durable too. *Real* durable. Most ain't.'

Philo returned his gaze, understanding perfectly. 'Yeah, you're right. Most ain't.'

Wilson swivelled on his stool. 'Let's call this fight off,' he said. 'There's no point to it.'

'I ain't doin' it for points.' Philo said, swigging at his drink.

Wilson looked at him and then laughed. 'Ah, you're good.' He shook his head then inhaled deeply, his smile fading. 'But you're not good enough. I – I don't wanna hurt you – an' that's the truth.'

'You know,' said Philo finishing his drink, 'sometimes we can't always do what we wanna do. Right?'

Their eyes locked. After a moment Wilson grunted. 'Yeah,' he said softly.

56

A bartender appeared beside them and looked meaningfully at the partially demolished table and chairs. The drunks had crawled off to tend to their wounds and bar staff were tidying up.

Wilson reached for his wallet.

Philo caught his arm. 'Your money's no good here,' he said.

Wilson withdrew his arm, smiling. 'Well thank you.' He stood up. 'A pleasure watchin' you work,' he said.

Philo returned his smile. 'Same here.'

Wilson hesitated a moment, then nodded and moved away through the crowd.

Philo sniffed, reached into his back pocket and deposited a wad of bills on the bar counter. The bartender scooped them up and went away.

'Who was that?' asked Lynne, leaning close.

Philo glanced at her. 'That's a friend of mine,' he said. 'We used t' play squash sometimes.' And, ignoring her quizzical glance, he turned to listen to the band, pushing worried thoughts far into the back of his mind.

CHAPTER 6

Philo ducked under the bonnet of the Pontiac Firebird, feeling some welcome relief from the noonday sun. He began tinkering with the twin carburettor, loosening nuts and screws at apparent random, letting his intuitive understanding of automobile engines some freedom to operate. The car – half wrecked as it was – had been an unexpected bonus for Clyde's high speed demolition work on the Mercedes. Orville knew a group of dragster fanatics who'd pay handsomely for the right kind of wreck. Philo had promised to take a look.

Clicking his teeth with satisfaction, he dug what appeared to be a hunk of oil-smeared horse hair out of an air channel, and flicked the debris into the junkyard. Apart from that, the carbs looked clear. He straightened up, squeezing his eyes in the sun's brilliance.

A pity all of life's problems couldn't be solved as easily, he considered, not for the first time that weekend. On the one hand he'd rediscovered in Lynne a joy he never expected to see again. On the other he stood an even chance of throwing it all way by letting Jack Wilson convert him to a basket case. But it wasn't even that simple. Now he had Lynne he needed the fight money much more urgently than before. And there was the question of pride too – the real reason, he knew now, that he'd accepted Beekman's offer. Wilson, quite simply, was the best. That was his reputation and, having seen him perform, Philo had no more doubts. They recognised each other as fellow professionals in one of the toughest, most vicious sporting activities on earth. Beating Wilson – Philo knew – had to be the summit of his career. Was that worth losing Lynne?

He heard a footfall on the Boggs' porch and looked up, shielding his eyes, to see her approach. She was dressed in neat, straight-leg jeans and a soft blouse and she looked good enough to eat. Philo's heart went gently bump, before he saw her grim expression. She stopped several feet from him, just as Orville slunk through the porch door and leaned awkwardly against a support post.

Philo frowned. This had every appearance of a showdown.

'I don't want ya to fight,' said Lynne.

Philo put down his car tools.

'You too. I thought you weren't supposed t' say anythin' t'her,' he called to Orville.

Orville looked unhappy. 'I thought she had more influence,' he said.

Philo sighed quietly.

Lynne's voice became softer, more intimate. 'Don't do it, Philo.'

Her eyes bore into him with a look that was as much warning as pleading. It was a soft blackmail – the more potent because it struck squarely at Philo's worst doubts. Instinctively he reacted against it.

'I'm doin' it and that's the end of it,' he snapped, snatching up a tool.

'But 'e *kills* people,' Lynne pleaded.

Philo turned to the open bonnet. 'The subject ain't for discusssion.' He snapped a spanner on a nut and applied pressure.

Nothing happened.

Lynne turned with a stricken look to Orville who shrugged helplessly. Behind him the insect screen slammed back with piledriver force and Ma Boggs stomped out of the house, head down and skinny arms swinging.

'Go ahead, *get* yourself killed, ya selfish lunkhead!' she bawled, shoving past Orville and making for Philo. 'Better still, let 'im scramble your brains so I c'n spend the next twenty years waterin' ya!'

She paused, quivering with outrage, as Philo stared at her. Then the horticultural reference reminded her of her flower garden which had only just recovered from Clyde's car-breaking exploits. She turned to it absently and cursed under her breath, seeing the orang-utan standing loose-limbed in the middle of it, his sad eyes glued on Philo.

'You too?' asked Philo.

The great ape slowly inclined his head.

Philo took a deep breath. It was a formidable barrage he faced. Elevating personal pride above the wishes of the only people in the world he cared for and who cared for him was hard.

Too hard for him.

He swallowed and admitted defeat. 'All right,' he said. 'All right, Clyde, go get the money. Go ahead.'

He let his breath go in a sigh as a smile spread on Lynne's face.

As the orang-utan ambled purposefully toward the house closely pursued by Ma – Lynne sprang happily towards him.

'Orville,' Philo called, reaching into his back pocket. 'Here's the card. Call that guy an' tell 'im t' come get 'is dough.'

Grinning, Orville sprang over and grabbed the crumpled business card as Lynne grabbed Philo. Beaming, she kissed him.

From inside the house there came a shriek of outrage. Ma Boggs hung in the doorway of her bedroom, gazing in amazement as an untroubled Clyde rummaged beneath her mattress, grunted in sudden approval and extracted ten thousand dollars in crisp one hundred dollar bills.

Ma smacked the side of her head in disbelief. 'Under my own mattress!' she gasped. 'Humiliating!'

Sniffing, Clyde lowered the mattress again and sauntered past her. She slumped against the door post.

'Out-smarted by a banana head!'

Patrick Scarfe was an unhappy man.

Unhappy at being roused from his bed, which he happened to be sharing with a shapely and deeply obliging young lady, at half three in the afternoon. Unhappy at having his hearing and competence savaged by a loud and even less happy James Beekman on the telephone. And unhappy at the experience of a violent electrical storm somewhere over Colorado which had caused the Eastern Airlines Boeing then whisking him from Kennedy to L.A. to imitate an express lift going up and down at the very same time.

Worse than that, though New York was shivering in an unseasonable cold snap, most of southern California – and especially L.A. – was doing quite the opposite, and Patrick Scarfe had had no time to revise his wardrobe. Sweating heavily in his three-piece worsted, despite arctic blasts from the air conditioning, he swung his light brown Avis Cadillac off Sunland Boulevard and headed at speed for the Boggs' homestead. It was night in New York, but still late afternoon in the San Fernando Valley as he skidded to a halt in the Boggs' driveway, in a swirl of dust and righteous indignation.

Philo was near the porch, tinkering with a car engine he had deposited on an old tree stump. He looked up in mild disinterest as Scarfe approached at speed, then looked back at his work.

'Hey!' Scarfe gave a loud whistle and stopped at Philo's side, his shirt unbuttoned and his face red and angry. 'I just spent the last five hours on a very bumpy airplane, Mr Beddoe! I'm not in a good mood!'

'Well,' said Philo, taking a firm grip on the engine and lifting it bodily, 'I don't blame ya.' He strode towards a makeshift work bench beside the Pontiac and lowered the engine onto it.

Momentarily disconcerted by this casual display of strength, Scarfe rushed after him.

'We have a deal, Mr Beddoe,' he said.

'We had a deal,' Philo replied. He picked up a rag and began wiping his hands. 'Clyde, get the man 'is money back.'

The orang-utan appeared round the front of the car and moved towards Scarfe, a wad of bills in his long fingers. Scarfe flashed him a worried look, then exploded. 'One does not cancel deals with James Beekman!'

Philo turned and frowned at him. 'One takes one's

61

money back. Or else Clyde gets bugged at one.'

The great ape thrust the money into Scarfe's hand, folding the man's fingers round it carefully.

Scarfe sighed, his cheeks trembling with rage. 'I am holding it for you, Mr Beddoe,' he cried and waved the bills in Philo's face. 'I will add fifteen thousand to it – an' give it to you when you show up for the fight!' His eyes narrowed. 'Bear this in mind, Mr Beddoe: what Wilson will do to you is nothing compared to what we will do to you if you don't show up for the fight!'

Philo tossed his hand rag aside. He'd shown the man sympathy.

That didn't have to include listening to threats. 'Clyde,' he said, 'escort the man out.'

He strode towards the house.

Clyde lumbered in Scarfe's direction. The small entrepreneur threw him a single horrified glance and backed rapidly towards his car.

'You will have a visit from some of my friends, very soon!' he called.

Philo stepped onto the porch. 'Will they be drivin' Cadillacs too?' he asked.

'Yes!' shouted Scarfe. He jerked open his car door as Clyde continued to amble after him. 'Long an' black!' he promised.

Philo nodded. He'd heard about Beekman's connections. They still didn't impress him.

'Clyde,' he threw over his shoulder, 'scrap the Caddie.' And walked into the house without a backward glance.

CHAPTER 7

Patrick Scarfe slammed the car door shut a fraction of a second before Clyde's bulbous grey muzzle filled the driver's window. He fumbled in his jacket pocket for the keys, dropped them, bent to snatch them from the floor and lifted his head to find himself staring at the foulest, most ragged set of teeth he'd seen in a long and far from uninteresting life.

Clyde smacked his lips together and gibbered happily at the appalling effect he was having. Then he ducked below the window and vanished.

Swallowing thickly, Scarfe stabbed the ignition key at its lock, and missed.

He cursed loudly. Why in hell hadn't he left the phone off the hook when he had feminine company? Good God, if a man couldn't keep his Sunday afternoons to himself what time could he call his own?

He stabbed again – just as a violent blow struck the front of the car. Immediately afterwards came the rending scream of tortured metal.

Scarfe gaped in horrified disbelief as the offside wing of the Cadillac jerked forward and leapt into the air – on the end of a long and hairy arm.

'Oh, Jesus!'

Icy fear trickled in his stomach. The car began to rock up and down on its springs, making any attempt to insert the ignition key almost impossible.

There was another violent jerk. The front fender shot several feet into the air and cartwheeled into the junkyard.

Inside the house Philo shrugged on a clean shirt in his room and glanced at himself in his basin mirror. He winced as the sounds of destruction filtered through the thin walls, followed by Scarfe's thin high screams. Buttoning the shirt, Philo paused a moment, considering whether to intervene. No, he decided not. Clyde hadn't had any decent exercise since the Mercedes.

Outside, Scarfe cowered in terror, his knees jammed in the Cadillac's footwell as Clyde, squatting on the wide bonnet, expertly removed the windshield. Hooting in triumph, he juggled the perspex from his hands to his feet, spun it gracefully and sent it whirling towards Ma's flowerbed. Then, with a gentle whoop, he hopped onto the roof. Scarfe peered uneasily above the gap where the windshield had been. Both front wings had gone and the bonnet was deeply indented. A buckled radiator grille lay at one end of it.

'Oh, Jesus!' he whistled, glancing overhead. He was grey and his hands were shaking. He needed both of them to slip the key finally into the ignition lock. He was about to turn it when the rear window flew out and what felt like a large steam hammer descended on the roof. The thunderous impacts continued until – to Scarfe's horror – he felt the roof fabric graze his scalp.

'Oh, God!' he wailed, flinging himself across the front seat. Between groans, he began to pray, gabbling the words and watching in mounting disbelief as the car roof sank to within a foot of the bonnet.

Up above Clyde grew bored with bouncing up and down, swung himself to the ground and nonchalantly tore the rear passenger door off. Only pausing to detach a sill, he moved on to the front passenger door and removed the window. Back in the house Philo tucked his shirt into his jeans, inspected himself in the mirror again and decided Clyde had had enough fun. Normally he was very gentle with people, but his excitement could easily get the better of him and he might take those gibbering sounds that Scarfe was making for encouragement.

Taking his time, Philo strode out into the hallway, through the house and onto the porch. He saw at once that he need not have worried. Clyde was standing just in front of the house, his shaggy arms raised in triumph. When he saw Philo he gave a joyful hoot and performed a slow and rather inexpert somersault, ending up on his back.

Philo nodded and grinned. Then he caught sight of the Cadillac and gave a soft whistle. It looked as if it had lost an argument with a compacter. Bonnet and boot tops were gone, so were the wings and wheel arches, all the doors and the windows; wires and interior fabric trailed everywhere; what remained of the bodywork seemed to have been hammered gently but enthusiastically all over. And in the middle of it, his body bent almost double, his eyes peering desperately through the thin slot which was all that remained for forward vision, was an ashen-faced Patrick Scarfe.

As Philo caught sight of him, he finally steadied his grip on the ignition. Incredibly the engine sparked and caught. Coughed, died, caught and coughed again. Smoke belched from the trailing exhaust. Then, rattling and banging, shedding hubcaps as it went, the shattered Cadillac crawled to the end of the driveway and, hiccuping loudly, dragged itself round the corner and out of sight.

'Clyde,' smiled Philo, 'you're real cute, ya know that?'

The ape blew a loud raspberry and grinned.

Orville sagged on a chair at the Boggs' kitchen table and gazed morosely across the room. He took a swig from a tumbler of Jack Daniels and burped gently. A doom-ridden KLAC ballad moaned from the portable on the breakfast bar behind him. Another goddam boring weekend.

With Philo out most evenings, he'd already spent a depressing number of nights on his emergency repair racket; he needed a break now. Nothing fancy. Just a few beers, companionable laughter, a place to unwind. Hell, even Ma was swapping dirty jokes with that gin-swigging old biddy who lived down the block.

And now Lynne was sitting outside again, waiting for Philo to slip into his finery for another evening of stars and romance. Orville sniffed, knowing he was being unfair but not letting it ruin his bait of self-pity.

It was the wrong moment for Philo to enter.

'Hey,' he grinned. 'How about we go up to Bakersfield

and mess around for a couple of days?'

'No thank you!' Orville gave a theatrical shrug. 'I'm not Clyde! I can't sit around eatin' bananas while you an' the broad're playin' pattycake!'

'Hey,' said Philo, 'she's not a broad.'

Orville's innate sense of justice welled up in him and turned his anger inward.

'Oh, that!' He sighed and toyed with his glass, 'Damn it, I'm just talkin' mad. You're allowed t' talk mad t' your friends! Ya know – if they are,' he added, throwing Philo a glance that was almost plaintive.

It made Philo smile. He sat down at the table picked up the half empty whisky bottle and poured himself a glass. 'They are and you're allowed,' he said.

'Shit!' Orville grinned sheepishly. 'She's a real nice girl.'

'I know,' said Philo, pleased. He swigged at his drink.

'Piece o' luck.'

'I think.'

'But I don't have t' like it,' Orville corrected, feeling he was overdoing this.

Philo frowned in instant agreement. 'Hell no. I wouldn't either.'

Orville looked at him warily. 'You wouldn't?'

Philo shook his head. 'Uh-huh.'

They stared at each other a moment, then broke into companionable chuckles. Friendly relations were re-established.

'Well ...' drawled Orville, 'maybe I oughta get really mad at ya then – '

He was distracted by Clyde shambling through the door and casting speculative glances at both of them. Philo reached out and ruffled his scalp. He gibbered an acknowledgement and peered at the table top.

'You better get goin',' said Orville, watching him, 'before he goes down the block again after that lady St Bernard.' He chuckled at the memory. 'Jesus, I never saw a dog turn grey overnight.'

Philo joined in the laughter, as Clyde stretched out an

arm, lifted the whisky bottle from the table, and upended it between pursed lips. 'C'mon,' Philo frowned, taking the bottle away and setting it down. He grasped Clyde's hand, as it swept across the table top in search of more items of interest. 'C'mon, that's enough. You'll get blasted before we reach Bakersfield. Let's go.'

Orville shook his head, grinning.

'You take care now,' urged Philo, making for the door.

Orville waved his hand. 'All right. You too.'

'OK, Clyde.' Smiling his goodbyes, Philo shepherded the great ape out into the hallway and towards the porch.

Outside, in the cab of Philo's pick-up, Lynne turned from the driving mirror, where she had been checking her face, as the screen door slammed. Philo and Clyde bowled onto the porch. Lynne smiled and moved across the seat. The smile was as much for herself as for the others.

It seemed impossible that barely a week had passed since she and Philo had got together again. Somehow their relationship seemed to exist outside of time. Every morning, when she woke, she felt like pinching herself to see if it was after all only a dream. Never before - except in snatched moments in a stranger's bed - had she entrusted herself so fully to someone else. And now the holy terror she'd felt, screwing herself up to make that commitment, seemed the dream, the nightmare she'd rather forget.

Clyde cracked open the door and bounded inside, settling beside Lynne. Philo bundled in after him, smiled in greeting and kissed Lynne on the cheek.

There was an instant hoot from Clyde. Bowing in apology, Lynne ducked her head and allowed the orang-utan to plant one of his sink plunger specials on the side of her chin. Philo laughed uproariously, switched on the engine and pulled out of the driveway. Turning toward Sunland, he accelerated smoothly down the block.

Coincidentally Philo and his makeshift 'family' were not the only individuals in the immediate vicinity to enjoy a moment of rare good humour.

As the Apache drew level with an empty property two

67

houses down, satisfied chuckles emerged from behind the clapboard fence that fronted it.

Instantly twelve grinning heads, rising as though from a crouched position, appeared over the top. Their eyes followed Philo's retreating tailboard hungrily.

There was a throaty roar as a dozen heavy motorcycles sparked into life. In a swirl of dust, fuel tank gleaming and riding crop erect, Cholla thundered out from behind the fence, closely followed by the unruly leering members of his pack. Bumping across the pavement and into the roadway, he wrenched on the throttle grip, his shoulders hunched forward and his pock-marked face splitting in a snarl of triumph.

He should have done this months ago. Just hoping to run into a wily snake like Beddoe was a waste of time; you had to search him out in his lair, choose the moment – and pounce!

That skinny little bartender at the Palomino had been so helpful about Philo's address, too – especially when Dallas and Bruno had sat on his stomach while Elmo threatened to drive his chopper over his neck.

Cholla guffawed at the mental picture. Wasn't he a mean mother, or *wasn't* he a mean mother? His eyes narrowed on his victim. Retribution was nigh.

Fifty yards up the road, Lynne allowed the day's single jarring note to surface in her mind. Deliberately, while Philo had tidied himself, she had stayed put in the pick-up. The reason was simple. The more Orville saw of her the more grim-faced he became. Lynne knew why perfectly well and resented it as much as it aroused her feelings of guilt. But it was still something she ought to clear up with Philo.

She let out a sigh, glancing quickly at Philo and wondering how to start.

Eventually, she said, 'Seems like Orville's not too happy these days.'

Philo nodded, without turning to her. 'I know. I guess he thinks you've taken up some of 'is space.'

'But I can't give it back to 'im,' Lynne said quickly.

'I know,' said Philo. He turned and gave her a swift, warm smile.

Lynne watched his face. There was no rancour in it. If Philo hadn't squared things with Orville yet it would be done very soon, without blame on either side.

Relaxing, Lynne smiled back and stroked Philo's shoulder gratefully. She was marvelling at how easy things could be, if only you let them. It was another aspect of the daily miracle that made up her feeling for Philo.

Wrapped in happiness, she was only vaguely aware of the thunder of motorcycles close behind them. It was not until Philo glanced in the rear mirror and clicked his teeth in annoyance that she took any real notice. Clyde, meanwhile, had twisted round to stare through the back window. He gave a hoot and raised his middle finger in a classic gesture.

Lynne turned to look. There was a pack of scruffy-looking bikers directly behind them. The overweight ugly one in the lead seemed oddly familiar. His teeth were bared in a savage grin and the pick-up appeared to have all his attention.

Something clicked in Lynne's memory. A roadside in Colorado. Her long flight from Philo. The tubby one had flagged her down, demanded to know Philo's whereabouts. With a threat of violence in his narrow, piggy eyes.

'Hang on,' said Philo suddenly. He yanked on the wheel and the pick-up swerved across the road, clipped a kerb edge and bounced into a side turning. It was a broad, concreted boulevard between parched suburban houses. A hundred yards ahead it curved left in a dog leg. Straight on it was sealed by a row of no entry signs, guarded by a road worker with a hard hat and an orange flag. Philo slammed into third, stomped on the accelerator and aimed straight for him.

Now, thoroughly alarmed, Lynne clutched at the door. Beside her Clyde leapt up and down, gibbering excitedly. She turned to glimpse the bikers wheeling in dogged pursuit.

As she looked back the road worker loomed frighteningly close, his mouth opening in a wide 'O' of disbelief, then terror. Before Lynne could catch her breath, he'd shrieked and dived sideways, his flag and helmet flying in the opposite direction. Then the windshield darkened in a hail of debris. A splintered length of notice bearing the word 'entry' stuck in the door mirror an instant, before clattering away.

Beyond, the good road surface vanished in ruts and grooves as Philo touched fifty-five, his foot still hard on the throttle. Instantly the pick-up imitated a cocktail shaker, a rattling thunder arising from its tyres.

Hanging on for dear life, Lynne caught sight of a road gang at work directly ahead. A heavy tanker blocked one side of the street, while a tar laying truck was angling to block the further side. Liquid blacktop gushed from its spray arm in a thick black curtain. Half a dozen men in hard hats were yelling and waving arms in protest. The gap between tar truck and kerb narrowed – fifteen feet, twelve, ten.

Lynne squeezed her eyes shut. Bumping and rattling, the pick-up shot through as the speedo needle flickered on sixty. There was a hissing roar, a wave of heat through the passenger window and a pungent odour. Then they were clear.

Opening her eyes, Lynne turned and looked back. The curtain of tar sealed the road completely. They'd missed dowsing or collision by fractions of a second.

Then she gasped as she realised the bikers were not so lucky. Exploding from the black curtain they skidded and swerved across the newly layed blacktop, each one swathed from head to tyres in a warm, treacly coat.

Her laughter drew Philo's eye to the rear mirror. He grinned at the bizarre sight. That should hold them for a while. Exchanging smiles with Lynne, he eased off the accelerator but kept up a steady fifty as the road curved into a lazy turn. Factory yards and outbuildings appeared on either side. The road narrowed.

Philo's smile faded as the curve suddenly straightened. Cursing, he slammed through the gears and trod on the brake. Jerking everyone forward, the pick-up skidded to a halt, inches from a high steel mesh gate, heavily padlocked. There was an empty lot beyond, factory walls to left and right. A complete dead end. Cutting the engine, Philo leapt from the cab and began quickly winding up his window. As Clyde sprang to the ground beside him, he reached under the seat for a tyre lever.

'Lock the doors,' he ordered a wide-eyed Lynne, and slammed the door behind him.

He stepped away from the pick-up as the Black Widow pack, now resembling two-wheeled and rather overweight tar babies, glided round the corner and drew to a sticky halt. Sucking in breath, Philo bunched his fists and steeled himself for the onslaught. Beside him an equally belligerent Clyde mimicked his stance.

One by one, eyes gleaming as they fastened on Philo, the Widows cut their engines, dismounted and propped their bikes. Yet to Philo's eye there was a slowness, a deliberation about each movement that seemed a little overdone, even for someone relishing a moment as obviously as they did. Suddenly a wail went up from a steer-horned figure on the left.

'Cholla - I'm hardenin'!'

Dallas of the Nazi helmet stood stockstill, his arms oddly tensed, his eyes darting wildly.

'I'm hardenin' too!' gulped little Elmo from the front rank.

Cholla snapped a scowl at him. 'Shut up an' get 'im! Move!' he snarled.

'I'm froze!' cried Dallas.

But Cholla's eyes, their whites blazing like beacons in his blackened face, were fixed on Philo. 'Dead meat, Beddoe!' he promised and cackled. 'Dead meat!' He pushed his right shoulder forward, both hand clutching an upraised crowbar. Nothing happened. The tar had set like a cast. Alarm showed in his eyes, then rage. He began to totter.

'Oh, you're gonna pay for this - ' An ebony statue, he toppled facedown in the dust, his crowbar still clasped before him.

71

'You're gonna pay!' he bawled.

One by one, as Philo gazed in astonishment, the Black Widows, immortalised in tar, clattered slowly and impotently to the ground. The last two to fall tumbled towards each other, locked shoulders and remained fixed, propping each other at a constant forty-five degrees to the vertical. With an incredulous grin, Philo turned to the pick-up where Lynne was laughing helplessly in the rear window. Unlocking the door, she hurried over to him.

'What are you going t'do with 'em?' she asked, stifling her chuckles.

'Well,' Philo considered, 'we can't leave 'em here. Dogs would come along and piss on 'em.' He walked over to Cholla and looked down at him. 'It ain't fair t' the dogs.'

'You'll pay for that, too, Beddoe!' rasped Cholla, his voice necessarily muffled by its proximity to the ground.

Clyde blew him a loud raspberry.

There was unusual activity outside the main entrance to the California Emergency Hospital that afternoon. Almost a dozen nurses and interns, who by rights should have been attending to more pressing duties, were crowded together beside the main doors, gazing at a patch of lawn in the forecourt and giggling in a manner close to hysteria. The object of their attention was Philo's pick-up – or, more accurately the dozen rigid and groaning figures who were being unloaded from the back of it by means of a mobile tow boom and a sling.

Deposited in an untidy mass beside a flowerbed, the Widows looked like a set of discarded black shop dummies, dressed by a designer with a deep loathing for humankind.

Philo swallowed his laughter and turned to the smooth-faced intern in charge.

'You'll be able to get this stuff off?' he asked.

'Sure.' The intern ticked a clipboard he was holding. 'We'll just peel 'em like bananas.'

Groans of alarm came from the prostrate bikers. 'Of course,' the intern added brightly, 'that tar'll take most of the hair off with it.'

'Oh.' Philo nodded. 'Painful?'

'Moderately.'

'Too bad.' Philo turned with a grin as Cholla swung past on the sling.

'Oh, you're *really* gonna pay for this, Beddoe,' he wheezed; there were tears of frustration in his eyes.

'I already am paying for it,' said Philo, reaching into his back pocket for a wad of bills. He peeled off two tens and handed them to a green-suited mechanic who was unhitching Cholla from his sling. 'It's twenty for this tow boom an' another twenty I'm addin' on for cleanin' up my truck. That's forty dollars ya owe me.'

He strode back to the pick-up, yanked open the door and climbed in beside Lynne and Clyde. Behind them Cholla's bellows of rage mingled with the moaning of his men and the giggling of the nurses.

CHAPTER 8

'We're gonna do *what*?'

Lynne looked at Philo incredulously. They were speeding down Interstate Five, coming up to Wheeler Ridge and the Bakersfield turn-off. Long shadows were stretching from the Pleito Hills to their left.

Philo turned from the highway ahead and smiled at her.

'It's easy,' he said. 'Zoos are for keepin' the residents in, not for keepin' us out. You'll see.'

Wide-eyed, Lynne searched his face for a sign that he was joking. Philo's smile was blandly genuine.

'Woo-eeee,' she breathed, sliding back on the seat.

'Hey,' said Philo. 'Clyde has needs too, ya know. Romancin' ain't just for people.' He ruffled Clyde's ruddy mane apologetically.

'Human people, I mean.'

The great ape grunted and nuzzled his arm.

Slumped in the seat, Lynne eyed then both, laughter in her gaze. Then she straightened up.

'But how do ya know there's a lady ape where we're goin'?' she asked.

'There's one,' said Philo. He turned and grinned at her. Lynne kept her face straight for brief seconds, then burst into gales of laughter.

'Clyde, you rogue!' she declared, nudging him with her shoulder. The orang-utan ducked his head and blinked shyly up at her.

'Hey, cut it out,' Philo laughed. He reached out an arm and pulled Clyde's head protectively against his side.

'C'mon now – you're embarrassin''im.'

It was dark when the Apache rolled to a squeaky halt, its engine cut half a block away, outside the main gate of the Bakersfield Zoo. The gate consisted of a tall iron grating under an ornamental arch; there were pay booths on either side. Jungle grunts, snuffles and the occasional roar echoed distantly over the buzz of the cicadas.

In the front seat Clyde was already getting restless, twisting round on his haunches and sniffing the air. Quietly Philo cracked open the door, took Clyde's hand and led him down.

'We should be back in fifteen, twenty minutes,' he told Lynne, closing the door on her. 'I hope.'

'Good luck!' she whispered.

Philo nodded and took Clyde to the gate. He glanced inside, then paused a moment, listening. If there were guards around they were keeping very quiet.

Philo bent his head toward his ape buddy.

'C'mon, Clyde,' he motioned. 'Scrap the gate.'

Reaching up, Clyde's massive fingers wrapped themselves around a substantial looking padlock. There was a single rapid crack, and the grating swung inwards.

With a wave to Lynne, Philo slipped inside, ushering Clyde before him. Pushing the gate to behind them, both figures vanished in the dimness beyond.

Lynne glanced up and down the entrance road. It was deserted. She sank back into the seat, shaking her head. Someone had better not come along. Vandalising zoo entrance gates might not be so bad, but Lynne was fairly sure that kidnapping and seducing a lady orang-utan would be very difficult to explain.

Inside Philo let Clyde take the lead. Weaving between the darkened animal enclosures, the great ape grew increasingly excited, whistling and hooting in anticipation and tugging at Philo's hand.

'Take it easy, Clyde,' Philo whispered, looking around. 'We don't wanna be disturbed now.'

But the great ape only hooted louder. As Philo winced, a faint but unmistakable answering hoot drifted on the night air. Clyde tensed, his head jerking round. The hoot came again. Gibbering happily, he dropped Philo's hand and loped round a dark corner.

Frowning, Philo hurried after him.

They found themselves facing the orang-utan enclosure. It was a high concrete island, decorated with rocks

75

and tree stumps, and separated from the spectators by a deep, steep-sided channel. Clyde swung himself up onto the guard rail and hooted plaintively across the gulf. Dark hairy shapes moved in the shadows between the rocks. The answering hoot came again.

Philo peered across at the island, straining his eyes. He could hardly pick out individuals in this darkness, let alone the newly arrived female who was the object of Clyde's attentions. But Clyde was going to have to sort out that little problem himself.

Philo reached into his jeans pockets, carefully extracting a flat plastic case and a slightly squidged banana. Tucking the banana under one elbow, he opened the case and took out a syringe with a round bulb at one end. It was an instrument designed specially for use with animals which Philo had picked up in a pet store in Pacoima. The liquid it contained – a quick-acting knock-out drug – had been more expensive, the result of prolonged negotiation and rather more dollars than Philo cared to remember via a cage cleaner at Jungle Land. It was actually intended for chimpanzees, but Philo had been in no position to quibble.

'Despite your irresistible charm, ol' buddy,' Philo murmured to a whistling Clyde,' she may have some reservations.'

He pricked the banana skin with the syringe needle and injected half the syringe's contents inside. Placing the syringe case on the parapet, he wheeled Clyde around and pressed the banana into one hand.

'So you just feed 'er this and it'll put 'er out,' Philo instructed him. 'Not more than about forty minutes, though. Now if that doesn't work – '

Clyde whistled again, his head swivelling back to the enclosure. Philo pulled him round again, demanding attention. He pushed the syringe into Clyde's other hand.

' – Just pop 'er in the ass an' squeeze the bulb. Got that?' Clyde regarded the syringe with sudden interest. He lifted it to his nose, sniffed it then plunged it into his leg, clutching the bulb at the same time. As Philo gaped at him, he gave a soft whistle, rolled his eyes and fell flat on his back.

Sighing, Philo raised his eyes skyward.

'Clyde,' he murmured, 'sometimes I think you're not too tightly wrapped.'

Lynne gave a jump as the entrance gate clicked open suddenly. Spinning round, she saw Philo lumbering under the weight of a gently snoring Clyde.

'Oh no,' she cried, pulling herself across the seat. 'What happened?'

With a grunt, Philo heaved the unconscious ape into the back of the pick-up and took a deep breath.

'I seem t' have the only primate in the country that's a dope addict,' he snapped. He reached into the back and picked up a coil of rope.

'Be right back,' he said and made for the gate again.

'Be careful,' Lynne called after him. Philo nodded and was gone.

Outside the orang-utan enclosure he tied one end of the rope securely to the guard rail, tested the knot then rummaged in the back pocket of his jeans. He dragged out a crumpled scrap of newspaper and unfolded it. It was Clyde's own pin-up of Bonnie, the zoo's latest ape acquisition.

Philo picked up the drugged banana from where Clyde had dropped it beside the parapet. He glanced from the newspaper cutting to the dim shapes in the enclosure opposite. In this light they could have been Sasquatches for all he could make out.

'Well – ' he sighed loudly. 'It's 'is own damn fault if I get the wrong one.'

And he tossed the banana to the nearest hairy outline.

The long black limousine purred quietly into the Boggs driveway and eased to a standstill a dozen yards from the darkened porch. Front and rear doors opened noiselessly and the four occupants stepped out.

Tall and muscular, their prizefighter faces at odds with the expensive three-piece suits they wore, they paused, eyes directed towards the lights in the house. Distant radio music murmured over the hum of the cicadas. Their leader, a shorter, dark-suited man with receding hair, turned and glanced round the junkyard and the deserted street beyond. Then he nodded, reached under his armpit and drew a heavy Colt automatic. All four men moved toward the front door.

The first to reach it tried the door knob, found the door unlocked and cracked it open. Then, at a nod from the leader, he gave it a sudden vicious wrench, slamming it back and tearing off one hinge. In the same instant he kicked at the insect screen beyond, sending it spinning across the hall.

The four men piled into the house, unholstering further sidearms as they went.

In the dining room Ma Boggs sat at the table, poring over a magazine. She'd hardly registered the destruction of her front door when the four hard-eyed strangers burst in on her.

'Who the hell're you!' she snapped.

'We're lookin' for Philo Beddoe,' said the leader.

'Well he ain't here!' Ma turned abruptly as one of his companions swept down the room and through the archway that led to Orville's den.

'Get outta my house!' she bawled, outraged.

Orville was slumped across his bed, drinking in the country sounds from his portable in a semi-doze.

He looked up, blinking, at the total stranger in the doorway. 'Who the hell are you - ?'

Expressionless, the man leaned forward and smashed him expertly and painfully in the jaw.

Groaning, Orville lurched sideways. The stranger grabbed him and yanked him to his feet.

Ma looked up with a gasp as Orville staggered through the archway, propelled by his attacker.

'That ain't him!' barked the leader.

Punched in the spine, Orville crashed to his knees across the table from Ma, his chin thumping on the tabletop.

'Where is 'e?' the leader snapped.

Appalled, Ma turned blazing eyes on him. 'Why don't you go f —!'

'Maaaaa!' Orville pleaded in a high-pitched whisper,

his round eyes pleading caution. He'd only just noticed the abundant hardwear.

'Where is 'e?' repeated the leader.

Ma's gaze wavered from him to Orville's desperate expression. He nodded furiously.

'Uh - Bakersfield!' she offered.

'Where in Bakersfield?' the leader barked.

Ma sniffed and looked away from Orville. 'I don't know.'

There was a soft click. Orville twisted his head and glimpsed the muzzle of an automatic inches from his left ear.

Ma's gaze had followed his; she swallowed. 'Uh - he's gonna find a motel when he gets there.'

Stepping away from her, the leader pushed Orville roughly to the floor, and moved quickly to the door.

As Ma gasped in protest, the man who had dragged Orville from his room bent and let fly with a sudden jab that snapped Orville's head round and laid him out cold. The man hurried out after his companions.

Wincing and gasping, Ma pulled herself to her feet and scrambled round the table. She got down beside Orville, shaking her head at the split in his cheek and the thin trickle of blood from the corner of his mouth.

'Oh ... oh,' she murmured. At least he seemed to be breathing. She ran her hands over his gently heaving chest. No broken bones either. Then her fingers snagged a key ring in his breast pocket. She lifted her head. If those musclebound gangsters were looking for Philo ... She bunched her fist, inadvertently thumping Orville's chest as she struggled to remember where Philo could have gone. Orville had mentioned it over supper. That motel Philo always used for his romantic liaisons - or so Orville had thought.

Philo hadn't actually said. *Orange Flamingo, Pink Flamingo* - she screwed her eyes up at the effort - *Pink Cloud*! That was it.

With a grunt of satisfaction, she snatched up the key ring and struggled to her feet.

Somebody had to warn Philo. Orville could sleep for

hours. She grabbed her handbag from the table and made for the door.

After all that effort to get a driving licence last summer she was actually going to use it at last. She bustled through the front door, reached automatically to close it behind her and saw it hanging by a single hinge.

'Son-of-a-bitch!' she growled.

Orville's tow truck was parked across the drive. A brand new Volkswagen hung from the tow boom. Orville had brought it in earlier on an intercepted Triple A call. It had a slow puncture in the offside rear tyre which Orville had pumped furiously in order to tow the car home. The car's own spare had been missing. The disgruntled owner had been dropped at the bus station.

None of this was known to Ma, who did not even notice the Volkswagen. She made straight for the cab and fumbled at the door wondering vaguely why it should have 'Duke's Reliable Repair Service' emblazoned on the side. Then she got the hang of the catch and hauled herself inside. She had never driven in the dark before and the cab light went out as soon as the door was shut.

She rummaged around the dash, cursing and wishing she'd brought her close-up glasses. Then, more by luck than judgement, the ignition key found its lock. The engine roared into life and she rattled through the gears, looking for first. Finding it, she pressed hard on the throttle. The truck moved forward sluggishly, sending up a low mechanical growl. Angry, she smacked the wheel and pressed even harder. Then she remembered the hand brake.

'Oh, c'mon - ' she told herself, and yanked it up. The truck rocketed forward, slewed round the drive entrance and bouncerd over the kerb. Swinging behind it, the Volkswagen connected loudly and spectacularly with a row of dustbins, demolishing one and scattering three across the roadway.

Ma ignored the racket and, clinging grimly to the wheel, accelerated up the block.

Behind her, the Volkswagen's nearside tyre - gashed by a jagged edge of dustbin metal - began slowly to subside.

CHAPTER 9

The desk clerk of the Pink Cloud Motel glanced up idly from his portable TV as the pick-up swung in off the highway and parked by room number nine. He hiccuped, leaned back in his chair and plucked an almost empty Bourbon bottle from under the small reception desk. He was a lean, grizzled man, well preserved for his seventy-odd years, if only by a liberal application of alcohol.

It had been a quiet evening – hardly four rooms taken. He could be safely soused within the hour, doze happily until morning. He took a swig from the bottle and replaced it, turning his attention back to the TV screen. Midget biplanes were machine gunning King Kong on the top of the Empire State Building. He did not appear to like it. The desk clerk grinned, feeling the whisky warm his gut. He loved these old monster movies. They were so utterly ridiculous.

Philo and Lynne climbed out of the cab and peeped in the back of the pick-up where the two orang-utans, now both fully conscious, were huddled together. Clyde's arm was draped protectively around his new love's shoulder. She blinked shyly up at the humans.

Lynne smiled at Philo.

'It looks like you got the right one,' she said.

'Yeah.' Philo smiled back and let down the tailboard. 'C'mon, c'mon, Clyde,' he urged.

Rising slowly, the great ape gripped his girl friend's hand gently and led her down from the truck.

The desk clerk chuckled again as Kong snatched a biplane out of the air and crushed it angrily to matchwood. 'Make a monkey out of *me*,' the clerk murmured. Distracted by an odd movement outside, his eyes lifted momentarily from the screen.

And bulged.

Two distinctly Kong-like figures were alighting from

the pick-up in the parking lot.

He blinked rapidly, a single fear-crazed thought darting through his mind. The DTs.

It had been a year since the last time. That had been pink alligators, pinky *furry* alligators.

He shivered at the memory.

Grabbing the station dial, he squeezed his eyes shut and switched channels. He opened his eyes again, and started.

Chimpanzees dressed as cowboys were wrestling outside a scaled down saloon.

Shivering, he switched again. A cartoon gorilla demolished two palm trees in pursuit of Tarzan.

His mouth gaped. He snapped off the set, feeling the sweat break out all over him. Swallowing, he turned slowly back to the parking lot.

It was empty.

'Evenin'.'

Philo's brisk smile loomed out of the darkness. It faltered slightly as the desk clerk lurched sideways in sudden fright. Philo stepped into the tiny office.

'I'd like two rooms, number nine and the one next door if they're free,' he said.

Wordlessly, the desk clerk dropped the keys into his hand and pushed the registration book forward.

'I'll sign f' my friends,' said Philo. He scribbled in the book, gave the goggle-eyed clerk a curious look and left.

The desk clerk took a deep breath, then reached forward and turned the registration book round.

His eyes glazed.

Philo had written: 'Mr & Mrs P. Beddoe and Mr & Mrs C. Kong.'

The third car in as many minutes roared past Ma Boggs with horn blaring and headbeams flashing. False teeth gritted, she swore at them silently.

Goddam rowdy drivers. Didn't they have anything better to do than harass an old lady? If she weren't in such an all-fired hurry she'd a good mind to pull over and report them to the cops.

A fourth car blared past. She blew a raspberry at it, then narrowed her gaze.

The sign for the Bakersfield turn-off reared out of the darkness. About goddam time. This tow truck had the speed of a lame tortoise.

With the speedo needle bouncing on sixty, she switched lanes, only afterwards remembering to glance in the rear mirror.

She gasped. Some goddam *idiot* was letting off fireworks on the highway! Sparklers all over the sky! With a shiver of disgust, she turned back to the road ahead. There ought to be a law.

Grumbling quietly, she sped towards Bakersfield. Behind her, tyreless now, the Volkswagen was down to its rear wheel hubs. There was a fresh shower of brilliant white sparks as the bumper made its first contact with the road surface.

Philo sprawled on the king size bed with his shirt off and listened to the hissing of the shower next door.

'Cloud Nine', as the label on the door described the room, wasn't in the super deluxe class, but the name had always appealed to him.

There'd been quite a few young ladies who'd found the invitation of an evening or a weekend on 'Cloud Nine' practically irresistible. But Philo didn't want to think of any of them now.

He looked up as the shower stopped.

Lynne stepped out of the bathroom, shaking loose her soft blonde hair. There was a towel tucked into her bosom. She smiled deliciously, relishing Philo's admiring gaze.

'Do you think Clyde knows what to do?' she said eventually.

'Well – ' Philo moved across the bed, making room, 'there've been primates around for eighty million years. I don't think they'd set that kind o'record without doin' somethin'!'

Lynne's smile broadened. She placed one knee on the mattress and leaned forward, her small high breasts mounding forward as her eyes raked Philo's bared chest. 'I guess not,' she breathed.

In 'Cloud Eight' next door Clyde had just discovered how the shower worked. He paused, listening to its hiss and enjoying the luxury of his own private rainstorm. Then he picked up a pink flowered shower cap, sniffed at it, turned it over several times and planted it on his head. He stepped into the shower, hooting with pleasure as he felt the droplets patter on the plastic of the cap. There was a long handled scrubbing brush in the corner of the shower. He picked it up, rubbed it experimentally against his teeth, then began dragging it through the lank, dampened hair over his belly. He gibbered contentedly. It was a good tingling sensation.

After a few moments he got bored. He turned off the shower and stepped out, dropping the cap and brush in the bottom. Through the damp heat of the air his sensitive nostrils picked up Bonnie's subtle female odours, and twitched.

This was no time to be fooling around in rainstorms. He snatched at a large towel and dragged it over his body, the way he'd seen Philo do it. Then, treading it underfoot, he ambled through into the main room. Bonnie was sitting up in bed, a sheet draped over her waist.

She blinked at him shyly and looked away, her long fingers clenching and unclenching against the sheet. Jungle instincts beat in Clyde's barrel-like chest. He somersaulted elegantly across the bed, ending up next to his lady love, leaned across and smacked a resounding kiss on her soft grey muzzle.

Breathing deeply as a shiver took her body, Lynne sank against Philo's broad chest, her lips moulding against his.

As they came up for air, loud thumps echoed through the party wall behind the bedhead.

'What is *that*?' said Lynne.

Philo grinned. 'It's just Clyde showing off. That's part of the courtship.'

'Oh.' Lynne threw back her head and laughed at the thought of Clyde going through a Tarzan act. It just

84

didn't seem his style.

Clyde, meanwhile, couldn't have disagreed more. As Bonnie waited patiently in the bed, he performed a series of slow somersaults around the room, bumping inadvertently against odd walls and pieces of furniture. On his second circuit he noticed the light fitting in the middle of the ceiling. With a hoot of joy, he leapt onto a low dressing table, tensed his limbs and sprang. His right arm caught the fitting. Hanging by it he swung wildly for a moment as plaster dust rained from above. In a moment his gyrations slowed and he found himself facing Bonnie. She was looking at the door. With a soft whistle Clyde brought her gaze back to him. He flexed his limbs and cooed.

It wasn't exactly a liana vine, but he would do the best he could.

The thin party wall that separated 'Cloud Eight' from 'Cloud Seven' acted much like a soundboard. Sleeping quietly in number seven, Luther and Loretta Quince were first alerted to the racket next door by an irregular vibration rising through the frames of their twin beds.

Then Loretta snapped open her eyes and sat up. Less than three feet away, on the opposite side of the walls Clyde had leapt from the light fitting to a heavy armchair. It reminded him of his favourite in the shed back home. He began to bounce up and down, cooing and grunting and throwing Bonnie covert glances to see how he was doing. The chair springs squeaked and groaned beneath him.

To Loretta's startled ears the rhythmic thumping resembled a mattress undergoing a merciless punishment. Clyde's deep-throated grunts only confirmed her worst suspicions. After a pleasant week recovering from her unspeakable first impression of the Golden State, they were sharing their motel with a sex fiend.

'My God,' she whispered, 'that's obscene!'

Luther opened his eyes and peeped over his bed sheet. He listened a moment.

'Sure sounds obscene,' he said, with interest.

Philo and Lynne surfaced again from an even longer embrace. Both were smiling. As Philo reached down and tugged lightly at the top of Lynne's towel there was a heavy crash from 'Cloud Eight'.

'Hey,' said Lynne pressing a finger against Philo's bare shoulder. 'Don't I get a courtship?'

Philo sat up. 'Well, wha'da you want me t'do?' he asked.

Lynne considered this. 'Well, I don't know. Show off a little.'

She half closed her eyes in her finest Lauren Bacall manner.

'Wha'da ya say, big boy?' she purred.

Arching his eyebrows, Philo drew in breath and rolled off the bed. He stood up, glancing round the room.

Lynne subsided in giggles on the pillow.

Then Philo's gaze alighted on the central light fitting. He threw a questioning glance at Lynne, who shrugged. Then he moved to the middle of the room, reached up, tugged experimentally at the fitting. Satisfied, he stood on tiptoe, took a firmer grip and let the fitting take his weight.

'How's that?' he asked, raising his legs and swinging on one arm.

Lynne pursed her lips, 'I'm impressed.'

Then she burst into gales of laughter. 'Will it hold both of us?' she asked.

Clyde was enjoying himself. Even if the frenzied thumping he was giving the armchair was doing it little good, he felt marvellous. The blood surged through his veins. His eyes sparkled. He looked at Bonnie. Her eyes showed a similar gleam. He had all her attention now. He gave a loud hoot of triumph.

Sucking in breath, Loretta Quince flung herself out of bed and across the room. She snatched a suitcase up from the floor, dumped it across a chair and snapped it open. 'We're leavin' this place immediately!' she announced. 'Get up!'

Luther watched her dreamily from his bed. The frame

86

was still vibrating under him from the force of Clyde's exertions next door.

My God, Luther thought. That man must be an animal. There was something magnificent, primitive in the sounds coming through that wall. It had been years since he had experienced passions like that.

His eyes sank to his wife's rear as she bent to retrieve a fallen garment. She wore a plain white shift and the bottom it covered was several inches wider than when it had first attracted his eye so long ago. But Luther didn't mind.

Its wiggles as Loretta struggled to catch hold of her lost clothes were in perfect time to the bestial pounding from next door. Jungle drums beat in Luther's ear. His blood was up.

'Ummmm!' He smacked his lips and rose from the bed. '*Savage*,' he mouthed.

He moved towards Loretta, his eyes never shifting from that bobbing bottom. He shuffled one way then the next, moving his arms and snorting. It was his conqueror's shuffle, his makeshift mating dance.

'Ha!' he laughed.

Loretta straightened and turned to him with a look of outrage. 'Luther!' she snapped. She'd never seen him like this before.

He laughed again, lasciviously, his hands clasping the back of a chair that blocked his path. He wrenched it ceilingwards, effortlessly, brandishing it like a victory trophy.

'Luther, stop that!' Loretta cried, genuinely alarmed.

'Ha!' Luther's lips spread in a snarl of lust. Spread – and froze.

His eyes grew round, his face pale. He was stuck fast. 'My back!' he gasped. 'I've thrown out my back.'

Swiftly, businesslike, Loretta took the chair from her husband's hands and set it down.

'Stretch your arms, Luther,' she ordered, massaging his back and forcing him to bend. 'Don't tense.'

Luther groaned and shook his head. 'Fool!' he snapped,

disgusted at himself. 'I should've known better.'

'It was very brave, Luther,' his wife assured him; she went on massaging his spine. 'That was a heavy chair.' Her soft tone surprised him. He half rose and turned to her.

'You looked very impressive,' she said. Her look was demure, almost girlish.

Luther's heart beat faster. He straightened, back pain forgotten. 'So did you,' he murmured, smiling.

Their hands met. 'It's been a long time,' Loretta said sweetly.

Luther's eyes darted toward the beds.

Two doors away, in 'Cloud Nine', Lynne finally let the towel loose at her bosom. Philo's gaze moved down her body. She reached out her hand toward him.

Next door Bonnie extended a hairy forearm towards a jubilant Clyde.

And in 'Cloud Seven' Loretta Quince lay back on her bed and offered her hand to her husband. Luther licked his lips and grasped it tenderly. They had a lot to catch up on.

In a phone booth beneath a highway-spanning sign that announced 'Bakersfield' the tallest of Ma Boggs' visitors flicked impatiently through Yellow Pages. Finding the Motels section, he ripped it out and marched back to the waiting limousine.

He climbed in and handed the torn sheets to the man in charge.

'How many?' asked a voice from the back.

'About a hundred,' snapped the leader. He turned to the driver.

'Let's go.'

So engrossed were Beekman's hirelings by these activities, none had noticed the Duke's Repair Service tow truck which had just zipped past them in a shower of sparks. The Volkswagen hanging behind it was down to the doors, and vanishing fast.

Orville groaned and opened his eyes, wondering for a

bizarre moment why his head was lying on the floor of the Boggs' dining room. Then he remembered and struggled to his feet. His head ached and there was an ominous silence.

He staggered through into the kitchen and splashed water on his face and neck, wiping himself absently with the net curtain.

'Bakersfield,' he murmured.

He hurried across the hallway and out onto the porch. An Oldsmobile, halfway through a new paint job, was parked just off the driveway. Flinging himself into it, Orville flicked the ignition switch and shot out into the roadway.

The problem was, the desk clerk decided, the DTs weren't normally that disciplined. They tended to come at you out of the walls and act in a generally devil-may-care manner. They didn't bid you good evening and quietly sign the register. His curiosity aroused, he stepped out of his tiny office and crossed the parking lot, tip-toeing as he approached 'Cloud Eight'. The light was on inside and there was a tiny crack in the curtain.

Glancing round, he ducked down and peeped through. At that moment Ma Boggs spotted the sign she was looking for, swerved across three lanes without a second's thought and bumped into the forecourt of the Pink Cloud.

There was no mistaking Philo's pick-up in the line of guests' cars. And no sign of any unwelcome guests yet, either, thank goodness.

Switching off the engine, she eased out of the cab and slammed the door.

As she moved away from the truck, the remains of the Volkswagen - the front axle and a twisted length of chassis - crashed to the ground. Ma clicked her teeth in disgust at the noise. Damn silly place to hang a pair of wheels.

Hidden by the parked cars, the desk clerk was having trouble getting a clear view of the occupants of room eight. All he could make out was a mass of flying bed sheets and the occasional pillow. Whoever Mr and Mrs Kong were they were certainly an athletic couple. He grinned at the thought. My God, it had been a while since he'd had some action like that.

'Hey, get away from there!'

He jerked round in surprise. A tiny, feminine figure confronted him in the shadows. Her eyes gleamed angrily. 'It ain't right t' watch folks go humpety bumpety!'

Whether it was the poor light or his own burgeoning imagination, the desk clerk didn't know or care, but passion surged within him.

'Heyyy, baby,' he growled, rising and stretching out his arms.

Ma kneed him sharply in the crutch. Her bony fist cracked his jaw. With a loud groan, he crumpled to the ground. Ma gasped and stepped back, clapping her hand to her mouth.

'Oh, my God, what have I done – ?'

She glanced upward.

'The first live one in twenty years and I disable 'im.' Bustling forward, she caught the desk clerk under one elbow and helped him to his feet.

'Ah, c'mon, sweetie,' she urged, dusting him down. 'Gee, that was just a little tickle t' loosen ya up, you know.'

He stared at her warily.

'Now I tell ya what ya do,' she smiled, pulling him back to the window. 'Ya get yourself a good eyeful. C'mon. Just look, look right in. Enjoy yourself.'

Still uncertain, the desk clerk glanced inside.

'And then when you're ready for a real romp,' Ma gave him a broad wink and clicked her teeth, 'I'll be in the office.' She winked again and turned away, waggling her hips. 'Roll me over,' she sang, 'in the clover. Roll me over, roll me over and do it again. Cha-cha-cha-.'

She threw a last smile at the astonished clerk and skipped into the shadows.

Thirty miles to the south Orville depressed the accelerator a further half inch as he roared onto the Bakersfield turn-off. The speedometer needle nudged eighty. Keeping a weather eye open for traffic cops, he prayed silently that Philo had decided on the Pink Cloud – and that Ma hadn't caught up with him.

Chuckling to herself in the confines of the motel store room, Ma shrugged off her thin cotton dress, her slip and her sandals. Then she looked down at her knickers and her old brassiere. No; she shook her head. She didn't want to frighten the poor fellow.

Casting round, she picked up a spare bed cover and wrapped it around herself. That was what she needed. Allure. Smiling, she peeped round the door into the office. It was empty. She shuffled through, noting with pleasure the little cot in the corner.

But it wouldn't hurt to ask for a little help.

She looked up at the ceiling.

'Uh, you know I ain't a church goin' person, but I swear – ' she raised her hand – 'that's gonna be a *thing* of the past.'

She paused. 'Let it be all right.'

She grunted and dropped her hand.

'I didn't hit 'im hard,' she murmured. 'He should still have one good one left.'

Something moved beyond the office windows. Ma tensed, straining to see.

The desk clerk formed out of the shadows. His face was glowing, his eyes shone, fixed on some radiant, erotic, inner vision.

He reached out towards Ma.

'Sweetie ...' she gasped, and cocked one eye skyward. 'Thank ya, Lord.'

Outside, a long black Cadillac slinked past the forecourt, and braked abruptly.

A head ducked out of the front passenger window, staring keenly at Philo's pick-up. Then the leader of Beekman's heavies consulted a slip of paper with Philo's licence plate number scrawled on it.

'That's it!' he cried.

The Cadillac swung into the forecourt.

Two blocks away Orville spotted a local police prowl car parked at the kerb. Its two officers were munching hamburgers at a cafe table on the pavement next to it.

Orville squealed to a halt beside them.

'Uh, say, excuse me, officer,' he called through the side window, 'can you tell me where the Pink Cloud Motel is?'

The largest of the two policemen spoke through a mouthful of burger.

'Yeah. Just hang a right out here. Go down a little bit a ways. Ya can't miss it.'

Orville nodded, lifted his cap and reversed it.

'Well,' he boomed, 'how'd you an' your girlfriend there like t' race me over?'

As the burger exploded from the officer's lips, Orville stamped on the accelerator and screeched away.

The Cadillac eased to a halt in the parking lot, blocking any access by the pick-up. All four doors opened quietly. While the two men in the rear turned to watch the office and the motel entrance, the leader and his driver drew guns and approached 'Cloud Nine'.

One block away, Orville weaved between two slower cars, touching sixty as he did it. He snatched a glance in the rear mirror. The pursuing prowl car had been joined by another. Sirens split the air.

'C'mon, guys, c'mon,' Orville hissed. Then he caught the edge of the Pink Cloud sign dead ahead.

Hand raised to knock at the door, the leader of the heavies paused as he heard the wail of the siren. He glanced at his henchmen. The sound was coming this way.

Holstering his gun, he gestured to the others to get back in the car.

They had just closed the doors when Orville swerved through the motel entrance, slewed across the forecourt and crashed into the side of a gleaming Buick.

As two police cars bounced to a halt behind him, he leapt out the Oldsmobile and yelled, 'Philo!'

The door to 'Cloud Nine' cracked open. Philo's head emerged. Orville stabbed a finger at the side of the motel.

Philo turned, just in time to glimpse a long black Cadillac slide silently out of view.

'All right, wise guy ...' cried the burger-less officer and grabbed Orville's arm. His partner grabbed the other.

'Which station?' said Orville as he was frogmarched to the car.

'Fourth Street,' snapped the partner. 'Why?'

'Fourth Street stationnnn!' Orville bawled.

Philo nodded and ducked back into his room.

Two rooms down, Luther Quince poked his head gingerly, and belatedly, round the doorpost.

'What is it, snookums?' Loretta cooed from the darkness within.

'Somebody's bashed into our car, honeybunch,' he reported.

'We c'n always get another car.' A hand plucked tenderly at his sleeve. 'Come back to bed, sweetheart.'

Beaming, Luther went.

CHAPTER 10

Despite all the exertions of the night before, Philo was up early the next morning. Leaving Lynne still sleeping, he shrugged on his shirt and jeans, pulled on his boots and stepped outside.

The new sun was still sending long shadows across the forecourt and the flickering Pink Cloud sign looked wan and gaudy. The air was cool and clear.

Philo strode to Clyde's door and ducked his head to it, listening. All was quiet within.

He moved across to the pick-up, dropped the tailboard and reached across to a long metal box half covered by a tarpaulin. He pulled the box to the tailboard. Its catch was padlocked. Fetching the key from his back pocket, he released the lid.

Inside, wrapped carefully in cloth, was a freshly oiled pump action shotgun. There was a box of shells next to it. He picked them both up, closed the lid and pushed the box back under the tarpaulin.

Glancing round him, he moved to the cab, opened the door and stowed shotgun and shells behind the passenger seat. Then, with a further glance about him, he closed the door and went back into 'Cloud Nine'.

Lynne smiled at his kiss then slowly opened her eyes.

'Hi,' she purred. Her arms rose about him.

'Hi,' he whispered, and kissed her again, more lavishly. He broke away with a deep gasp.

'I'd love ta make this last,' he breathed, 'but we're gonna be in big trouble if Clyde doesn't get his ladyfriend home.'

'Oooh.' Lynne's lips pursed in a mock sulky pout. 'You sure ya couldn't manage just five little minutes ...?'

Her eyes widened innocently as she stretched her arms, forcing the bed sheet to slip below her bosom.

Philo's gaze fell. He gave a long, low sigh.

'Five medium-sized minutes?' he suggested.

An hour later Lynne was driving the pick-up down back roads towards Bakersfield Zoo. Clyde and Bonnie huddled in the back.

Philo was unwrapping a long, cloth-wrapped parcel. He lifted the shotgun free and began loading it with shells. Lynne glanced at him in alarm.

'What's that for?'

Loading complete, Philo ran a cloth over the breach and tucked the gun behind his seat.

'Just in case,' he said.

Loath as he was to admit it, he could have done without Lynne's company for a while. He'd expected trouble from Beekman, and was confident of holding it at bay until the man's resentment had cooled off. But having Lynne along was an added complication.

The pick-up turned down a service road at the back of the zoo. It drove between ragged borders of shrubbery, curved past a dense clump of underbrush and came to a high wire mesh gate. A sign read: Gate 2 Service Entrance. Lynne cut the engine and braked.

Philo climbed out and went over to the gate. It had a simple slide bolt holding it shut. There was no padlock. He glanced inside. Nothing moved among piled crates and tubs of animal feed. Loosening the bolt, Philo moved back to the truck and let down the tailboard.

'Here, take 'er home.' He beckoned to Clyde. The great ape rose to his feet and shambled down the truck with Bonnie in tow.

Philo helped them both down. 'Hurry on back,' he urged.

With a grunt, Clyde led the way through the open gate.

Philo returned to the cab, glancing round. Then he tensed. Disappearing noiselessly behind the clump of underbrush he glimpsed the boot of a long black Cadillac.

He eased open the cab door and lifted the shotgun from behind his seat. Lynne looked at him with a questioning frown.

'You wait here,' he told her.

Before she could reply, he'd gone, skipping lightly across the concrete and ducking into the underbrush close to the gate.

He moved quickly but carefully, half crouched, working his way toward the further side.

Dry brushwood crackled and snapped up ahead. Philo stiffened, then sank slowly onto his haunches, his shotgun upraised.

However awesome they might appear on city streets, the two smartly suited heavies were no woodsmen. They moved awkwardly, forcing away snagging branches with the heavy automatics they carried.

They were totally unaware of Philo until he rose silently behind them, pumping a shell into the breach with a loud click. There was no mistaking that sound. They froze, lifting their arms and letting their guns fall to the ground.

'Over this way,' Philo ordered, nudging their backs with the shotgun muzzle.

The heavies stumbled despondently onto the concrete in front of him. Glancing from left to right, Philo maintained a discreet distance as he urged them toward the side of the pick-up. It looked as if this was going to be a lot easier than he'd anticipated.

Then they drew level with the cab.

A small, thick-set, dark-suited man was squeezed in tight against Lynne. He was pressing a cocked automatic against her temple.

She stared at Philo, terrified.

The man grinned wolfishly. 'That's enough!' he barked.

Turning with a smile, the tallest of the heavies snatched the shotgun from Philo's limp fingers. He swung the stock smartly upwards, catching the side of Philo's head. As Lynne gasped, Philo grunted and slumped to the ground.

'C'mon!' rasped the small man, dragging Lynne through the door.

The Cadillac reversed swiftly from behind the clump of

underbrush and halted beside the pick-up. The driver, chewing the end of a thin cheroot, leapt out and opened the rear door as Lynne was bundled inside. Then he turned to the pick-up, lifted a handgun from a shoulder holster and blew a hole in the front tyre, only inches from Philo's head. He shifted his aim to the gasoline tank and fired again. Tossing down the butt of his cheroot, he jumped back into the now crowded Cadillac. It shot away immediately.

Gasoline trickled from the holed tank in a steady stream. At first it collected in a widening pool a yard from Philo's boot. Then the liquid struck a slight depression and funelled off across the concrete. The still smouldering butt lay directly in its path.

There was a soft *whoomph* and one side of the pick-up vanished in sudden flame. Then the cab window cracked and the seats took. Fire boiled across the dashboard. In a few seconds the whole truck was an inferno.

Clyde negotiated the last of the animal feed tubs and paused, his nostrils twitching at the stink of burning in the air. Then he saw the orange flicker of flame. Puzzled, he moved closer, sliding round the edge of the gate. The pick-up had gone. In its place was a huge burning thing of fire and smoke that sent out waves of heat. His nostrils twitched again, in apprehension. And then he saw Philo. Inexplicably he was lying down, almost beneath the burning thing. Already there were wisps of smoke rising from the shirt on his back.

Frightened as he was, Clyde recognised danger when he saw it. His big hairless buddy had picked the wrong place to fall asleep in.

With a gibber of defiance at the fire thing, he leapt toward Philo, grabbed his arm and began to drag him back towards the gate. He was grunting and panting by the time they got there.

Philo's eyelids flickered. He sat up, blinking and shaking his head. Then he felt Clyde's arm on his shoulder.

He patted it, smiling, as he realised what had happened.

'Thanks ol' buddy,' he said. 'That took guts. I owe you.'

Clyde nuzzled his chin, gibbering happily. Then both of them jumped as the overheated gas left in the tank reached ignition point. With a thunderclap roar the pickup blew apart, and a broiling mushroom of flame soared sixty feet into the sky.

It was noon before Philo reached Bakersfield's Fourth Street police station. The taxi fare from Bakersfield home had taken half his ready cash. But he'd been relieved to see Orville's tow truck parked in the driveway. Then puzzled to find Ma sitting dumbly inside, gazing through the windshield with a beatific expression on her face. His attempts at conversation on the journey back to Bakersfield had not met with success.

Wondering vaguely about shock, he'd left her in the truck while he and Clyde went into the station to pay Orville's bail. That had taken the rest of his cash.

Now all three emerged onto the station steps. Clyde dropped Philo's hand and looked meaningfully towards a parked patrol car.

'Don't even think about it,' Philo warned.

They piled into the tow truck beside Ma. She turned to them with a saintly smile then gazed distantly through the windshield.

Orville frowned at Philo.

'How long has she been like this?'

'All morning.' Philo shrugged. 'Ain't said a word.'

They drove off.

They had reached Interstate Five before they had pieced together the events of last night and this morning.

Orville swore as he learned of Lynne's kidnapping.

'I suppose you'll have t' fight now,' he told Philo.

'Yeah.' Philo nodded grimly.

'I don't think they're actually gonna hurt 'er,' Orville offered. 'I think they just want ya t' fight. That's all.'

He glanced at Philo warily, trusting this thought was some crumb of comfort.

Philo seemed unmoved. 'I know,' he said.

'A piece o' crap, though,' Orville added.

'Yeah.'

Orville sighed and turned to Ma. Her expression had not changed. She seemed to be contemplating some beautiful memory.

Orville turned back to Philo.

'She's gettin' on,' he said quietly. 'Think maybe 'er brains're - you know - turnin' soft?'

To everyone's astonishment, Ma burst into song. 'Jelly, sonny, jelly. Jelly roll killed my mama, drove my daddy stone blind!' She chuckled happily.

'You're going t' church next Sunday,' she told Orville and raised a hand to the sky. 'You too,' she said to Philo, and lifted another hand.

She seemed quite determined.

CHAPTER 11

Philo tightened the last nut on the old Ford's cylinder head and straightened up from the open bonnet. He wiped his forehead in the dry heat of late afternoon.

He'd stripped and reassembled the engine in record time, but in a kind of thoughtless dream. The work hadn't been urgent, or even necessary. It was simply his own, well-tried method of dealing with doubts and worries. With a sigh he put down his wrench. This time it didn't seem to work too well. There was nothing he hated more than feeling helpless.

Across the junkyard Orville stumbled onto the porch. 'Philo!' he spluttered. 'It's him!'

Philo sprinted toward the house. The phone was on the breakfast bar in the kitchen. Breathless, he snatched it up. 'Yeah?'

'Jackson, Wyoming. Saturday, noon,' Patrick Scarfe intoned crisply.

'Not until I talk to 'er,' Philo rapped.

Scarfe's tone deepened. 'You are in no position t' set conditions, friend.'

'You heard me,' said Philo.

Some two hundred miles due east Scarfe glanced across the Nevadan Motel suite. Three of the Beekman heavies sat round a coffee table playing poker. A bedroom door was open beyond them. Scarfe picked up the phone and moved across to the doorway.

Lynne sat against the bedhead, the leader of the heavies in a chair at her side.

'Dino!' Scarfe snapped, motioning to an extension phone on the bedside table.

The leader picked up the phone and handed it to Lynne. Lifting his automatic, he moved closer to her.

'Philo …?' she asked tremulously.

'You okay?' Philo asked.

100

'I'm fine. Look,' she said with more confidence than she felt, 'don't fight, they don't dare hurt me.'

'I trust you are not so foolish as to believe that, Mr Beddoe,' Scarfe barked into his own receiver.

'No, I'm not,' said Philo. 'Lynne, the fight's not your concern. I'll have you outta there on Saturday.'

'Philo,' Lynne began, 'listen to ...'

Scarfe nodded quickly and the receiver was wrenched from Lynne's grasp.

'We have a deal, Mr Beddoe?' he asked.

'Yeah,' Philo replied grimly. 'You'll produce 'er Saturday, noon, before the fight - right?'

'Deal,' said Scarfe. He slammed the phone down.

As darkness fell, Cholla's Harley chopper swung into the driveway of the Widows' Pacoima stronghold, negotiated a pile of discarded tyres and halted beside the bikers' eleven other machines.

Propping his cycle, the leader of the pack lifted a large cardboard box off the gasoline tank, glanced surreptitiously around him and scurried inside. It was a wholly uncharacteristic entrance, but not without justification.

As he burst into the cluttered living room, the assembled Widows looked up in sudden alarm. Then relaxed as they saw who it was. Cholla smiled, safe from the eyes of the world. He contemplated eleven dully gleaming eggheads, hand plucked scalps from which even the eyebrows were missing. The Widows looked like contestants in a ludicrously postponed beautiful baby contest.

It was not a pretty sight.

'All right, boys,' Cholla beamed, turning to a dining table in the corner of the room and upending the box he carried. 'Belly up to the table an' get yourself some hair, there.'

As the grateful Widows surged forward, a dozen ill-made wigs in a variety of bizarre shades, from green to luminous pink, tumbled across the table top.

'And here,' Cholla added, reaching into his pockets and

tossing a handful of eyebrow pencils onto the heap, 'paint on some eyebrows. Ya look like a bunch of freaks!' He cackled happily as a general melee ensued. Not a bad deal for ten dollars. It had been pure chance he'd noticed that theatrical costumier on Van Nuys going bust the week before.

'Heyyy!' whined Elmo, rifling among the goods. 'You promised me a moustache.'

Woody, one of the eldest Widows, adjusted a Bo Derek wig over his eyepatch.

'Hey!' boomed Dallas, hornless for once. 'Cholla promised me I could be a blonde!'

He grabbed Woody's wig. Behind them more tussles developed.

'I wanna be a redhead!' Elmo complained.

Cholla's smile slowly faded. He watched in growing disbelief as the scourge of the San Fernando Valley battled over several ounces of garishly dyed horsehair.

'Hey, Cholla!' cried Dallas, his head trapped beneath Woody's arm. 'Why don'tcha tell 'em t' give me what I asked for?'

Cholla's eyes closed on the scene. His lips moved in a wordless prayer.

Next morning, for the second day in a row, Philo rose at dawn. Shadows of fatigue ringed his eyes as he loaded Orville's two truck for the long trip east. He'd been up till the early hours, chasing up every underworld contact he could think of and calling at a selection of the area's more remote and less fussy motels. It was no surprise to him that the task had proved fruitless. Beekman's men hadn't struck him as locals, nor foolish enough to hide out on Philo's own ground. But he'd owed it to Lynne to make the effort.

Over a breakfast of strong black coffee, he was joined by Orville, who had spent the previous evening in enquiries of his own. His dull-eyed expression showed he had had no more success.

They'd collected Clyde and were rolling through San

Bernadino's commuter traffic, en route for Interstate Fifteen, before their conversation developed beyond the level of nods and grunts.

Orville gave a long sigh. 'Nobody knows nothin',' he announced. 'I checked everybody I know, even the sleazies.' He grimaced at the memory of the Valley's skid row.

'Well, they're probably holdin' 'er somewhere near Jackson,' Philo replied, his gaze steady through the windshield. 'We'll just do a little scoutin'.'

Something in his tone caused Orville to glance at him. There was a coldness in Philo's gaze, an edge that Orville recognised. The last time he'd seen it Philo had been about to lay a fight-winning blow on Joe Casey. However tough these Beekman heavies would prove to be, Orville did not envy them.

Bareknuckle fighting receives little media coverage in the United States. You won't read about it in the best known newspapers or magazines. Sports commentators don't wax eloquent on the pros and cons of each contest on networked TV. The names of its stars would be unfamiliar to the most dedicated fan of Ali or Frazier or Sugar Ray Leonard.

But, within minutes of Philo agreeing to fight, the news had flashed across the country. Eastward to Beekman in New York where the word passed up and down the eastern seaboard. South to the beaches and bayous of Miami and New Orleans. North to Chicago, Detroit and Minneapolis. And west, to Houston and Dallas, Tucson and Albuquerque. Wherever men – and women – savoured challenges that smacked of pioneer days, or gambled at odds no racetrack or Vegas casino would accept, the word was heeded.

This, so it said, would be a big one. Between a killer and an upstart; a man who'd destroyed two lives and a fighter – so the rumour went – who'd run rings round the legendary Denver Tank Murdoch – then let the ageing champion win his match from sheer respect alone.

By the evening of Philo and Orville's departure the

fight was common knowledge round the bars and dives of the San Fernando Valley – dives so low that even the Black Widows were welcome.

As the news trickled past Cholla's bewigged ears, he chuckled into his beer. This had to be the opportunity of a lifetime. A chance to see that ape-loving knucklehead get pummelled to a pulp – and to win money on the result! Barely restraining his excitement, Cholla scuttled out the bar and back to the clubhouse. Whoops of wild joy disturbed the night. Within twenty minutes, bedrolls wrapped and engines roaring, the pack was on the road. There wasn't a moment to lose, and besides, looking the way they did now, the Widows only felt safe on home territory well after dark.

With a cat nap on the outskirts of Las Vegas, they'd reached the Utah border by late afternoon. They lunched on burgers and beer in St George and headed on towards Cedar City.

There was national parkland on either side, curving hillsides and banks of pine woods. The road was quiet too. Well-fed and well-oiled, Cholla felt a need to swagger. He gave the order to spread across the highway. The bikers' speed climbed to sixty, then seventy.

A siren wailed behind them.

The two Highway Patrolmen had had a quiet day. Two 10-46s, a 10-54 and a suspected 10-70, which is to say: a couple of broken down cars, a runaway heifer and a fire outbreak which turned out to be a picnicker's campfire in the wrong place. So the sight of a dozen Hell's Angels hell bent on disrupting the peace of the State of Utah seemed like the answer to a prayer.

Dutifully the bikers peeled off the highway into a layby, and the patrol car slid to a halt behind them.

Taking his time, the eldest of the officers – a lean, middle-aged man in sunglasses – retrieved his notebook from under the dash and climbed out the car. His partner joined him as they began a slow, steady walk down the line of bikes. It was immediately apparent that something was dreadfully wrong. Under the officers' disbelieving gaze, the Widows shifted awkwardly on their saddles, their eyes darting away as they tried vainly to readjust their windblown wigs. The patrolmen exchanged glances. They began to find difficulty in breathing.

'Oh Jesus,' whispered the elder. His face was pink, his lower lip quivering, as he reached Cholla.

His partner suddenly turned away and doubled up with the agony of restraining gales of laughter.

'Now why don't you just shut up,' snapped Cholla, 'an' start passin' out them tickets there.'

To his horror, the elder patrolman simply shook his head. He turned away, pushing his sniggering partner back towards their car.

'Ain't got the heart,' he muttered. 'You've got enough trouble.'

He began to splutter; his partner was weeping.

'Wait a minute!' barked Cholla, pursuing them. 'You have t' give us those tickets! You have to!' Distraught, he indicated the Widows with his riding crop. 'I mean, didn't ya see us? We're lawbreakers! I mean, we are *totally despicable*!'

Gasping, the officers stumbled away from him.

'We have *earned* them tickets!!' He gaped after them as they tumbled into their car.

'Son,' the elder called back to him through the open door, 'you are a walking violation of the laws of nature. But we don't - ' temporarily overcome he fell back into his seat - '*we don't enforce them laws!*'

He gave himself up to hysterical laughter. The car weaved back onto the highway and sped away.

Cholla stared after it, appalled. Slowly his arms spread, his chin lifted skyward.

'Lord,' he declared, 'you have *given* me these crosses t'bear an' I will carry them - all the way from Jerusalem t' Jackson, whichever's closer. But hear me, Lord - though I walk through the valley of the shadow of death, I will chew on Philo Beddoe's ass - for my last supper!'

His words echoed round the heedless pines.

It was late afternoon when James Beekman's feeder flight from Cheyenne banked high over the Rockies affording him a spectacular view of the Grand Teton mountain range directly ahead. Seven thousand feet of snow-flecked volcanic rock face, it rose sheer from the tranquil valley of Jackson Hole, America's premier ski resort. But neither scenery nor the prospect of firm snow occupied Beekman's mind. His attention was focused entirely on the town of Jackson some dozen miles to the south.

It had been a comfortable flight west and he was feeling good.

Everything about this contest seemed to be turning out right.

The fact that Wilson hadn't fought in almost a year only seemed to have whetted the gamblers' appetites. And this Beddoe character obviously had a good following on the West Coast. Bets were pouring in.

There were some high spenders who'd been wary after the last Wilson bouts. With the excitement brewing on this one, it might be worth making a few calls.

Beekman smiled to himself as the aircraft manoeuvred for its final approach. All his life he'd been looking for the one big shot, the ultimate set-up, which, if it paid off, would catapult him into clear blue skies, the Florida beach villa, the New Jersey mansion, a casino or two in Vegas. Security, legitimacy, respectability. He was getting that buzz in his nerve ends which told him this might just be the one.

He was chuckling when he met Patrick Scarfe at the barrier at Jackson airport. They shook hands warmly. Scarfe, who'd driven in that morning with Lynne's gaolers, seemed to have succumbed to the cowboy atmosphere already. He was wearing a western-style suit with a bootlace tie.

'This place is jumpin', Jim,' he enthused. 'I think we're onto a big one.'

It was what Beekman wanted to hear. Slapping his assistant's arm, he followed him out to the forecourt. A taxi was waiting.

'Ya got us somewhere nice?' Beekman asked, climbing in.

'Ramada Snow King,' said Scarfe, piling in behind him and tapping the driver's shoulder. The car drew away. 'The best.'

'But of course.' Beekman laughed and lowered the window a fraction.

He breathed in deeply. The skiing season had ended, but the mountain air was still crisp and clear. Beekman sighed and slumped in his seat. 'Any problems?'

Scarfe shook his head. 'Smooth all the way. We got the girl stashed – '

'Hey.' Beekman frowned, nodding faintly toward the driver.

'That's your business, OK? Don't bother me with details.'

'OK, Jim. Sorry.' Scarfe stiffened.

'Yeah.' Beekman glanced out the window. Then his good humour reasserted itself. 'We're gonna be busy tonight; we gotta lot o' calls to make.' He turned and grinned at Scarfe. '*Expensive* calls.'

To all outward appearances, Zachariah Hamilton Lee, plump forty-five year old owner of one of the largest and richest oil fields in West Texas, was a man in dire straits. He was down to his vest and his jockey shorts and all he held was a pair of twos and a Jack.

Luckily he had one or two extras in reserve – the wide, grey stetson on his head and the sunglasses on his nose. Which was more than could be said for his three female companions who lounged about the drawing room floor of Fat Zack's River Oaks mansion in a disturbing disarray of scanty underwear.

'Your call, Zack,' prompted Little Melvin, a diminutive business associate. His eyes gleamed behind fashionable steel spectacles.

He'd done rather better than most.

'I think ya got Sweet Sue worried here.'

A bubbly blonde in a fetching pink bra subsided in

giggles in the middle of the carpet.

'Well now - ' drawled Zack, lifting his gaze from the cards, and relishing the moment. A petite brunette and a statuesque redhead regarded him in mock alarm.

'What I'd truly like t' call for - ' He paused as the ladies' eyes widened ' - is a song from Long John there!'

Laughter and cheers swept the room. Squatting at the side of a huge, natural stone fireplace, Long John - a shirtless cowboy in his early thirties - snatched up a twelve-string guitar. With a loud 'Yippee-I-Ay!' he launched himself into a self-penned ditty on the exploits of one Cow Patti.

Wild applause greeted his invention.

Behind Zack the door to the hallway quietly opened. A sedate English butler, who seemed less than happy with his rhinestone suit and bootlace tie, entered with a telephone on an extension lead.

'Excuse me, sir, there's a call for you,' he announced, bending to Zack's ear. 'Mr Beekman.'

Zack's eyes brightened. Second to strip poker, James Beekman's wild contests were the gambles he loved best.

'Hellow, Beeky, it's your dime!' he boomed into the receiver.

'Zack!' The familiar tones came bright and clear over the thousand miles distance. 'I got a sporting event laid out for this Saturday. A fire-eater named Philo Beddoe.' He laughed lightly at the unusual name. 'Against Jack Wilson.'

'Philo Beddoe?' Zack queried. 'Never heard of 'im.'

Covering the mouthpiece, he ducked his head swiftly toward Little Melvin. 'Hey, Melvin, can Beddoe whip Jack Wilson?' he snapped.

Little Melvin looked sceptical. 'Beddoe's good. Real good. But I'd have t' give Wilson the edge.'

'How big an edge?'

'If it was my money, seven t' five. But six t' five is a fair bet.'

Zack uncovered the mouthpiece.

'I might be interested in four t' one,' he declared airily.

Little Melvin grinned and shook his head.

'Even money, Zack,' Beekman responded tolerantly.

'Well – ' Zack's drawled disinterest was theatrical. 'I might go three t' one.'

There was a smile in Beekman's voice. 'I've reserved your suite for you.'

Zack beamed. 'I'll be there,' he snapped down the receiver.

Across the room Long John's song rolled to its end with a triumphal 'Yippee-I-Ay!'

Zack took the cue for an even louder rebel yell. 'Ya all saddle up, everybody,' he announced. 'We goin' on a trip!'

A few minutes before midnight, Beekman took his first break of the evening and slumped down with a sigh on his hotel suite's long couch. Grimacing at the remains of dinner on a low table in front of him, he fumbled for a cigarette.

'Hey,' called Scarfe excitedly, slamming down the extension phone on the other side of the room. 'Jim Martin an' his crew are comin' in from Kansas City.'

'Yeah?' Tiredly Beekman lit up and took a deep draw.

'Yeah. We got contingents comin' in from Seattle, L.A. – an' Frisco.'

Scarfe's unabated enthusiasm revived Beekman slightly.

'Any takers at six t' five?' he asked.

'Uh-huh.' Scarfe nodded. 'We got about thirty grand. You know, Jim, we might have t' go two t'one if we wanna pick up the action a bit, uh?'

'No.' Beekman shook his head and drew again on his cigarette. 'We'll get enough action at eight t' five.'

'All right.' Scarfe sounded disappointed; it wasn't like Beekman to play it so safely.

'All right, I'll call up Boston an' set up a layoff.' He reached for the telephone.

'No!' Beekman spoke so quickly he almost spat out his cigarette. He leaned forward, snatching it out of his mouth.

'No. There's not gonna be a layoff.'

His weary gaze fixed on Scarfe, who blinked back at him in momentary disbelief. There was something very wrong here.

'Jim ...' He rose and moved across the room. 'Jim, we're liable t' get a couple o'million bucks on this fight.'

His tone was conciliatory, almost fatherly. For all its weariness, Beekman's stare did not waver.

'Wilson's not going t' lose,' he said flatly.

Scarfe gaped at him a moment, then laughed quickly. 'Now, we try any funny stuff here – ' he spread his hands. 'They're gonna retire us – to the Jersey flats!'

Beekman shook his head and returned to his cigarette. 'No, no; no funny stuff. I'm tellin' ya, Wilson's gonna take 'im!'

Scarfe sighed, blinking rapidly. Beekman had always been the one to take on the wildest, the most improbable bets but he'd never thrown away all the safety nets before.

He tried again. 'Jim – all we gotta do is set up a little layoff ... You an' me, we take a nice six, seven per cent cut. We walk away with a couple o' hundred grand. No risk.' The more he talked the more reasonable it sounded.

Beekman's stare was ice cold. 'I'd rather walk away with a couple o' million,' he said.

It wasn't just the journey and the evening on the phone which had made him tired. It was the effort of coming to the most momentous decision of his business life. He'd felt it in the air as soon as he arrived; he'd seen it in the faces of the gambling fraternity already crowding the hotel. This *was* the big one, the one to stake it all on. Win or lose. And the thought scared him half to death.

'Yeah – ' For a moment Patrick Scarfe was lost in his own dreams of the ultimate killing. 'Yeah, all right,' he said eventually. 'All right, I go along. But if Wilson loses – ' He aimed an accusing look at Beekman. ' – you better have snowshoes, 'cos north of the Artic Circle is the only place we'll be safe.'

CHAPTER 12

The taxi glided to a halt in the forecourt of the Ramada Snow King and Jack Wilson stepped out. As the driver struggled to lift a bulging shoulder bag and a suitcase that contained several of the fighter's favourite exercise weights from the boot, Wilson stretched his limbs in the morning sunlight. He breathed deeply, feeling the bite of the mountain air in the bottom of his lungs.

In other circumstances this might, he considered, be a great place to unwind. He sniffed at the thought and snatched up his baggage.

Wilson and Philo might be equals in ferocity in the ring, but out of it, their attitudes were as different as chalk and cheese.

Philo took a new fight as he took life, in his stride. Wilson trained with all the dedication of a legitimate professional. He worked and lived and slept with the thought of his opponent until only that person's annihilation could give him peace. And the fact that it was a man he liked and respected this time only made the process that much harder.

He pushed through the entrance doors into a crowded lobby. Immediately he was attracting attention from every side. Heads spun, whispers flew about the room.

Stone-faced, Wilson headed for the reception desk, only to find his way blocked by a beaming, bespectacled under-manager.

'Welcome t' Jackson, Mr Wilson, welcome!'

He blinked deferentially behind heavy black frames. Only the fact that Wilson had almost trodden the smaller man underfoot prevented him, it seemed, from wringing his hands in sycophantic glee.

'It's a great honour t' serve you, a *great* honour,' the man burbled on. 'I'm going t' take you up to your suite myself. Here – ' he clutched at Wilson's suitcase – 'let me

111

take this.' Obligingly, Wilson let it go and turned toward the stairs. The suitcase descended with a thump on the carpet, almost dragging the startled manager with it. With a momentary look of panic, he used both hands to lift it scant inches above the pile and shuffled in Wilson's wake, manfully attempting to reconstruct his welcoming smile.

'Uh, there are presently three parties in progress, one of which started yesterday afternoon.' He chuckled meaningfully. 'If there's anything you need, anything at all - ' his eyebrows rose and his eyes flitted conspiratorially from side to side. 'The hotel does allow *pets* in the room,' he announced in a stage whisper. 'If you understand my meaning ...'

He looked like a prurient high school student taking his first *Playboy* home carefully wrapped in a copy of the *Christian Science Monitor*.

Wilson's look was withering. 'I don't *keep* pets,' he said. And snatching his suitcase back strode quickly upstairs.

Conscious of the continuing stares of the other guests, the under-manager gave a simpering smile, reddened and hurried on.

Perhaps he shouldn't have ordered quite so many flowers as he had for Wilson's suite.

Several blocks away Orville's travel-grimed tow truck swung off the highway and pulled into a motel of low, timbered chalets, built to resemble pioneer log cabins.

Dozing in the passenger seat. Philo cocked an eye at the neat walkways and the well tended flowerbeds that bordered them. He'd heard the Tetons were expensive, but a place as touristy as this smacked of a loose regard for his hard earned dollars. He changed his mind when he entered the reception office.

The desk clerk was rangy and pop-eyed with a three-day growth of beard. Sniffing and spitting into a well placed spitoon, he growled out a price that struck Philo as the high side of average, but not unacceptable. As Philo counted out the bills, the clerk jerked his chin at a roughly scrawled notice on the wall.

'No pets. No booze,' he snapped.

'I c'n read,' Philo replied.

'And no parties.'

Something caught the clerk's attention through the open door at Philo's back.

Clyde was climbing laboriously down from the tow truck's cab. He was wearing an ankle-length dress and a large flower bonnet which covered most of his face.

It was a precaution Philo had thought wise to adopt after leaving California. They had picked up the clothes in Las Vegas after a fitting session which had left an elderly assistant in a state of nervous collapse. Clyde had accepted his disguise gracefully, though the bonnet had been replaced twice. In some dim recess of his simian mind, it seemed that the fabric of cheap bonnets and the seating material used in police patrol cars had an unfortunate correspondence.

'Oh, that's Aunt Hortense,' Philo said, following the desk clerk's gaze. 'The last party she was at was Teddy Roosevelt's inauguration.' He glanced quickly at the clerk, trusting his inspiration of the moment sounded more likely to the other man than it did to him.

Deep furrows grooved the clerk's brow. 'She your aunt by blood or marriage?' he asked.

'Blood,' said Philo. He pushed the money across the desk and hurriedly scribbled in the register.

The clerk shook his head. 'I'd be careful about havin' any children if I were you.'

Philo exited with a smile. 'Always am,' he said.

The entrance hatch of the private jet clicked open and two sober-suited businessmen stepped down, laughing and joking onto the tarmac of Jackson airport. Passing two boilersuited baggage handlers, they scurried across the field to the small terminal building. The shortest of the handlers watched them go, and whistled softly through his teeth.

'That's the fifteenth private jet this mornin'. What the hell's goin' on?'

His companion bent to the open luggage compartment.

'Bare knuckle fight,' he said, dragging out the first case. 'A California boy named Philo Beddoe is takin' on some monster from the east coast.'

'I ain't seen anythin' in the papers,' the other queried.

'Strictly illegal.' The handler turned and dropped the case onto a baggage trolley. 'No referee. An' the fight won't end until one or the other's half dead.'

As he swung back to the plane, a flash of reflected light from the sky caught his eye. He looked up.

'Jesus God ...!'

Sweet Sue was having difficulties. Worse than that, she didn't know why.

She'd been driving her daddy's tractor at the age of ten and she never had any problems with automobiles. So why couldn't Zack's twin engined executive jet be just as simple?

As they made their third pass across Jackson, she turned warily to Zack in the co-pilot's seat beside her. 'I think I'm doin' somethin' wrong,' she said.

Whoops of glee came from the two couples behind them. But Zack just gave her a broad smile. 'Well, you're doin' just fine, hon,' he declared.

Sue chewed her lip nervously. 'Yes, but we've been flyin' upside down for fifteen minutes, Zack.'

Hoots of merriment erupted from the back. Zack reached upwards and picked up his cigar butt which had been resting on the ceiling.

'Well, it just takes a little time t' get the hang of it,' he said. 'Don't be so hard on yourself.'

One seat back, Candy, the statuesque redhead, turned to Long John. 'Ya know, it's like that ride at the fair where everything falls out,' she grinned.

The cowboy's eyes fastened greedily on her low, bulging bodice. 'I hope so!'

Candy exploded into laughter. 'Oh, you're terrible!'

Behind her, Honeybun, the brunette, watched Little Melvin struggle with an inverted bottle of champagne.

114

'Hey, you can't drink upside down,' she told him.

'Oh sure you can,' Melvin smiled. He tucked the bottle mouth under his upper lip and carefully swigged a mouthful.

Candy and Long John gave a burst of applause.

'Here, try it,' Melvin offered.

'All right.' Grinning, Honeybun took hold of the bottle and folded her lips round the mouth.

'Hey!' she spluttered. 'It works.'

'Oh, you'd be surprised what you c'n do upside down.' Little Melvin leaned closer with a lascivious grin.

'Surprise me,' Honeybun cooed.

'Ohhh!' Melvin roared with enthusiasm. 'That's talkin'!'

In the co-pilot's seat Zack gently nudged the rudder bar. He beamed encouragingly at Sweet Sue as the jet turned slowly for its fourth pass.

Philo and Orville has stayed the previous night at Pocatello in Idaho, some hundred miles short of Jackson, and left at dawn to give themselves a full day searching for Lynne. Orville, it was decided, would use the truck. Philo would jog.

Within minutes of stowing their gear in the motel chalet, Philo had slipped into his training shoes and was ready to move.

'I'll take the south side o' town, you take the north,' he said at the door.

'What're we lookin' for?' Orville queried.

Philo shrugged. 'I don't know. Just keep your eyes out for anything peculiar.'

He nodded back into the chalet where Clyde was rolling happily about the largest bed.

'And keep Aunt Hortense outta sight.'

Orville nodded as Philo turned away, breaking into an easy running stride.

Even without the ragged peaks of the Tetons soaring to the north, Jackson was conspicuously a mountain town. The buildings were low and balconied, with wide broadwalks and a generous scattering of log walls - either genuine or meticulous facades.

The windows of small stores were piled high with ski goods and sportswear, hiking equipment and hunting rifles, numberless bills offering every kind of outdoor amusement, from climbing to trout fishing, chuck wagon meals to whitewater canoeing. There was even a cigar store indian.

Little of this registered with Philo. He'd enjoy the tourist attractions when Lynne was rescued and the fight won - and preferably after the first deed had been accomplished. He had scant respect for deals made under duress.

He turned into a broad avenue - and immediately saw the long, black Cadillac gliding into a public parking slot on the further side of the street.

Philo didn't hesitate.

Sprinting across the roadway, he snatched at the rear door, wrenching it open and drawing back his left fist.

Two little old ladies blinked at him in alarm. Dressed in pink and white respectively, yet facially indistinguishable, they could only be sisters.

Philo's face sagged. Feeling foolish, he dropped his arm.

Instantly the nearest lady - who happened to be in pink - gave a broad smile. 'Why, you're Philo Beddoe!' she exclaimed.

Philo looked at her uncertainly. Until now he'd been unaware of any geriatric branch of his fan club. 'Yes, ma'am,' he said.

'It's *him*,' the pink lady whispered gleefully to her sister. The lady in white jostled behind her for a closer look.

Her growing smile faded as she saw Philo more clearly. 'Oh …' she said. 'Why, he's lookin' too *good* …'

Philo blinked at her.

'Oooh, yes,' murmured the lady in pink. She unshook a golden handled lorgnette from her handbag and studied Philo closely. 'Oooh, too good by half.'

116

Philo's look became quizzical. 'Execuse me, ma'am.' He started to back away.

'We can't get decent odds on ya lookin' that good,' the pink lady explained. 'We're trying' t' find some *fool* who'll give us two t' one.' She laughed brightly.

Her sister leaned forward, nodding at Philo. 'Try t' look a little more peaked, would ya?' she suggested.

'Yeah.' Philo swallowed a smile. 'Excuse me,' he said, and jogged back onto the road.

He shook his head as he ran. He'd had no idea his popularity spanned such a wide spectrum. He wondered whether he ought to feel flattered.

Then his mind snapped back to Lynne. This was getting him nowhere fast.

He had turned a corner and was moving toward the centre of town before he became aware of the soft engine purr at his back. He threw a glance over the shoulder. A darkened windshield was less than fifteen feet behind him, the grille below unmistakably Cadillac.

Even in a fashionable resort like Jackson, Caddies weren't that thick on the ground.

Without warning, he peeled off suddenly to the left, reached the car in a couple of swift strides and yanked at the front passanger door. The car bumped to a stop and a male figure opened a mouth in protest behind the shaded glass. But the door was locked.

Unthinking, Philo punched at the window glass. It shattered spectacularly and he knocked down the handle inside, reaching through the empty window space and the opening door to drag the occupant outside.

Philo found himself clutching the corpulent bulk of a middle-aged man in stetson and sunglasses. A cigar stuck out the side of his mouth.

'Oh,' said Philo. 'Sorry.'

Somehow this wasn't turning out to be his day.

'You damn fool!' bellowed Fat Zack, struggling out of Philo's grasp. He clutched at the other's arm. 'Let me see that hand! Wiggle your fingers – '

Uncomprehending, Philo unclenched his right fist.

Peering at it, the bulky Texan breathed a deep sigh. Two more stetsoned figures climbed out the car, gazing anxiously in Philo's direction.

'Oh my ...' murmured Fat Zack. He snapped at Philo: 'You could've broke that hand an' made paupers outta all of us!'

Philo gave him an odd look. Before he arrived he'd thought some of the folks back in California were a little wild, but they had nothing on the average man in the Jackson street.

'Sorry about that,' he said.

Zack grunted and looked up. 'Well, wha'da ya standin' around here gabbin' for?' he boomed. 'Get on back t' joggin'!'

'Yeah.' Philo nodded vaguely. 'Think I might do that.' He turned away.

'Oh, and no booze, no parties - in bed by eight o'clock!' Zack called after him.

Philo waved a hand behind him. 'You c'n count on that,' he said.

'I do,' murmured Zack. His anxious expression lightened into a broad smile as Little Melvin and Long John joined him.

'Did ya all see that?'

'Yeah,' said Little Melvin.

He watched Philo's retreating figure in undisguised admiration.

'The way he grabbed me!' Zack chuckled explosively. He draped an arm over each of his friends' shoulders and hugged them. 'With one hand like I 'as a feather!'

Chortling happily, all three gazed after Philo.

'Son of a gun, boys,' yelled Zack, 'we're gonna be rich!'

Whoops of joy rent the quiet mountain air. Then they paused for breath.

'We're already rich, Zack,' Little Melvin remembered.

Philo heard the light footsteps behind him as he turned into the next street. Jack Wilson was wearing the same dark blue tracksuit he had worn at their first meeting.

'Mind if I jog with ya?' he echoed, matching strides.

Philo glanced at him stonily then away. 'You work for some pretty strange folks,' he said.

'Who I work for is my business,' Wilson replied.

It was seriously but not harshly said and Philo thought he detected a questioning note.

'They got my girl,' he snapped.

He caught the faint lightening of Wilson's expression. So the man didn't know, or gave a good impression of not doing so.

But that still didn't get Lynne back.

They emerged onto a wider street, passing beneath the balcony restaurant of the Jackson Hole Bar-B-Q Motel. Late breakfasters and early lunchers mingled at the open air tables. It was only a second or two before a check-shirted man at the parapet glimpsed the two joggers below.

'Hey!' he gasped aloud, turning so fast he spilled his coffee. 'They're runnin' t'gether!'

Half a dozen diners leapt up from their tables and pushed to the side of the balcony. They included the restaurant's white-capped chef.

'Jesus,' he whistled, 'talk about beef on the hoof.'

'Wilson'll eat him for *breakfast*!' grinned check-shirt.

'Well, I got forty on Beddoe,' countered a tall young guest, leaning past him for a better view.

'You're on,' snapped check-shirt.

Below, Wilson and Philo trotted out of sight.

'I didn't know,' said Wilson simply. He sounded suitably sympathetic and Philo acknowledged his effort, if only mentally; only results would make him happy this morning.

'I didn't say ya did,' he conceded. 'I just said you work for some strange folks.'

Wilson sniffed. 'Well, their business isn't mine.'

There was resentment in his tone.

'Never said it was,' said Philo.

They approached a junction.

'We're even,' said Wilson. He gave Philo a pointed look. 'Remember?'

And before his opponent could answer he wheeled off into a side turning and sprinted rapidly away.

James Beekman sprawled back on his hotel couch, pushing the remains of a late and substantial breakfast across the low table in front of him. One thing he could never deny himself - triumph or disaster, bouts of wild elation or crippling nerves - was good food. He'd gone without too many meals in his early days to let the least of the day's meal breaks pass uncelebrated. On the far side of the room Patrick Scarfe was answering a phone call.

'Oh, yeah,' He sounded uneasy. He replaced the receiver. 'Oh, Jim,' he said. 'Tony Paoli's on the way up.'

Beekman laughed indulgently and shook his head. 'Poor little Tony. He never learns.'

'Not Junior,' Scarfe hissed, scurrying across the room. '*Senior*.'

'*Big* Tony?' Beekman's face grew pale. He struggled forward. There'd been no news from the Don since the rattlesnake fiasco in New York. He'd been meaning to set things right, to soften the son's betting blunder with a few diplomatic moves. But the Wilson fight had come up too quickly.

'*Big* Tony,' Scarfe confirmed. He began shoving the food debris out of the way. Nervously, Beekman climbed to his feet, torn between giving Scarfe a hand and buttoning his shirt.

'Well, what's he comin' here for?' he asked himself. He reached for his suit jacket, dragging it awkwardly across his shoulders. His question was entirely rhetorical. No good ever came out of a personal visit from a premier New York Don - especially when the visit took him nearly two thousand miles out of his way.

There was a sharp knock at the door. Buttoning his jacket, Beekman nodded the Scarfe to answer it. Both men were sweating.

'Good morning,' Scarfe declared brightly.

A tall, dark-suited man in his fifties gave him a patrician stare and pushed past into the room, his eyes sweeping about. A beefier, but no less voluble companion, entered behind him, kicking open doors to bedrooms and the bathroom and ducking his head inside. Swallowing, Beekman looked on helplessly as the two bodyguards completed their search. Then the taller one turned back to the door and nodded.

Anthony Paoli Senior entered at a fast pace, making straight for the most comfortable armchair, which a bodyguard eased politely behind him as he sat. The Don was a short, powerful man with the heavy features, the broad jowls of a Mediterranean peasant, an impression countered entirely by his immaculately tailored pale grey lounge suit. He was wearing dark glasses of a stygian blackness.

Beekman settled onto the couch opposite him, straining to catch some expression in their dimness.

Paoli Senior exuded power and danger in equally intimidating doses.

'Aaaah, Mr Paoli!' Beekman smiled nervously. 'What a pleasure to see you.'

To Beekman's added consternation, the Don made no reply, simply raised his right hand and snapped his fingers crisply. The eldest bodyguard thrust a hand inside his jacket, a movement that brought Beekman close to cardiac arrest. Producing a thin solid silver case, he extracted a small cigar, clipped the end with a cutter he brought from a trouser pocket and handed the cigar to Mr Paoli. The Don placed it between his lips and waited.

Seizing his chance, Scarfe dragged a lighter from his pocket and, thumbing it furiously, thrust it in the Don's face.

A fraction of a second later, and with practised ease, the beefy bodyguard extended his own lighter. Ignoring Scarfe, the Don inclined his cigar to the second flame. Coughing, Scarfe withdrew, glancing awkwardly at Beekman whose forehead was already starting to glisten.

The entrepreneur plucked a handkerchief from the

couch at his side. He clutched it unconsciously in both hands.

Settled, Mr Paoli removed his cheroot with one hand and his sunglasses with the other. His eyes were dark and bright. He was smiling, a wide, friendly smile that chilled Beekman to the marrow.

'I hear ya ain't layin' off any of the action?'

'Well no; no, not so far. No, sir,' burbled Beekman, his head bobbing, undecided whether to nod or shake it.

Paoli's smile broadened. To Beekman it was positively tigerish.

'You got guts. I admire a man with guts.' He leaned forward, prompting a nervous jerk from the other.

'So I says – Big Tony – maybe now is the time you go out an' make a little bet with this high roller, Beekman. With guts.'

With a brief pause for effect, he raised a single finger. Beekman swallowed.

'A hundred thousand?' he whispered.

Paoli Senior chuckled silently, his gaze flitting to each of his bodyguards, whose lips curled upward mirthlessly. 'Mr Beekman – ' The Don spread his hands. 'You an' I are not men who deal in *five* zeros.'

'Ooh.' The soft groan was Patrick Scarfe's. He ducked his head toward his employer. 'He means six zeros, Jim.'

The Don's smile was beatific. 'He means six zeros, Jim,' he mimicked.

Slowly, as the Don's eyes continued to bore into Beekman, a nervous chuckle was forced from the other's lips.

'Of course I ... I have t' cover it, huh?'

Beekman dabbed at his forehead with his handkerchief.

The Don chuckled back. 'Of course,' he laughed. And laughed, and laughed, his eyes as dark as the muzzles of the guns bulging beneath the armpits of his bodyguards.

CHAPTER 13

Orville bundled the discarded hamburger wrappings together, crunched them into a round parcel and tossed them across the chalet into a waste bin. Then he took a final swig of his beer and regarded Philo silently. The fighter was sitting hunched over on the side of his bed, staring moodily at the wall, a half empty soft drink bottle in his fist.

They'd hardly spoken two words since returning to the motel for the evening. In terms of searching, it had been a fruitless day for both of them. There were a thousand motels and rented cabins in the Jackson area and almost any one of them could be a candidate for the kidnappers' hide-out. Two men alone wouldn't cover them all in a month.

'Tell ya what,' said Orville. 'Bars'll be warmin' up round now. I'll do a little wanderin'. Somebody's bound t' have heard something.'

'Yeah.' Philo visibly shook himself, drained his bottle and made to stand.

'Hey,' chided Orville. 'You've got some serious sleepin' t' do. Leave this one t' me.'

The door of the bathroom banged open and Clyde ambled through, his rumpled dress now looking somewhat the worse for wear. Bonnetless, he hooted at the two men in friendly manner.

'Oh shit,' mouthed Philo, seeing his bare head. 'That's the third one in two days.'

'Don't fret,' countered Orville. 'I stuck it on the wardrobe, outta harm's way. Hey, let me take Clyde along. He's been stuck in here all day.'

The great ape shuffled over to Philo and nuzzled his head against Philo's shoulder. Grinning, Philo ruffled Clyde's ruddy scalp.

'No, he'll hold ya up. We'll take a turn outside before I bed down. Won't we, boy?'

Clyde grunted softly and smacked Philo on the lips.

123

'OK, then. 'Long as ya *do* sleep,' said Orville. He opened the chalet door.

'Good luck,' Philo told him.

Orville nodded and went. Outside the tow truck started up and rolled away. Philo sat quietly as silence fell, punctuated only by Clyde's grunting and snuffling as he checked under his dress for fleas. Philo was teetering on the edge of depression – a mood he usually did not tolerate. He was ninety per cent certain Scarfe would honour the deal and produce Lynne as promised. But that small chance of disaster worried him more than he liked to admit. He realised that Lynne's absence over the past few days troubled him a good deal more than his injured pride. It had been years since he'd allowed himself to feel so vulnerable.

'Shit,' he murmured.

He was letting himself sink. He needed something to do.

Turning to Clyde, he prodded him lightly in the shoulder. 'Hey, ol' buddy, how's that right o' yours?' he asked.

Instantly Clyde brightened, abandoned his flea patrol and swung a hairy fist at Philo's chest. It connected with a thump, pitching Philo back across the bed. But in a second he had recovered and was pummelling at the ape's barrel-like body. In reply Clyde clutched at him with one elongated arm, while he beat at Philo's side with the other. So engaged, orang-utan and human rolled happily about the bed before crashing heavily onto the chalet floor.

'Woo-eee!' gasped Philo breathlessly. 'You're gettin' better every day, Clyde.'

The great ape gave a satisfied hoot, draped an arm over Philo's shoulder, squeezed hard then somersaulted backwards across the floor.

Laughing, Philo climbed to his feet. He and Clyde hadn't had a proper work-out since Lynne had returned. His moodiness had quite cleared.

He caught sight of the edge of the bonnet peeping over the top of the wardrobe at his bed side.

'Here, Clyde,' he called, moving round the bed and reaching it down.

The great ape shuffled back to him. Philo tucked it securely on the great, red-haired head, and laced it under Clyde's grey muzzle.

'I know it looks damn silly, but we don't wanna go frightenin' folks, do we?'

Clyde grunted without conviction. Philo stepped back, studying his ape friend. Clyde blew a raspberry.

'Clyde,' Philo warned. The great ape ducked his head. 'Now I'm gonna have a shower. You sit tight and we'll take a stroll in a minute or two.'

Clyde watched silently as Philo strode into the bathroom, kicking the door shut. In a moment there was a hiss of running water.

The orang-utan grunted and tugged at his bonnet. It slipped a few degrees more onto the back of his head. Bored, he began to circle the room, picking at bed sheets, the corners of drawers and suitcases. Until he reached the door.

It had a latch of a type Clyde hadn't seen before. His long dark fingers toyed with it curiously. It lifted and clicked down into a different position. To his delight, Clyde found the door swinging open towards him.

He poked his muzzle into the dimness beyond, sniffing at the heady, unfamiliar mountain air. This looked distinctly promising.

He waddled outside.

The desk clerk of the chalet motel padded wetly from his cramped bachelor quarters through into the reception area, his tall, flabby body wrapped loosely in a threadbare bathrobe.

He'd just had his week's shower and he was feeling horny. In fact, he decided as he rifled the cluttered cupboard beneath the reception desk, he was feeling *damn* horny. Out of season – especially right out here on the edge of town – this place was a morgue. It'd been a week since he'd seen a half decent female; one on the good side of forty, that was. The only guests had been three travelling salesmen, two fellows taking up jobs locally and a Baptist Minister. Not to mention the weird-looking biddy and her relatives today. He shivered at the memory. They just had to be mountain folks.

Then his beady eyes brightened

By God's good fortune one of those guys passing through had unwittingly abandoned a pleasant little treasure trove. Just for him.

Chuckling with glee, he scooped up three well-thumbed copies of *Playboy* and deposited them on the desk top. He whistled softly as he flicked through the pages of the top copy.

That Baptist Minister had sure been a horny devil.

'Sweet, sweet honey,' he whispered, unfolding the centrespread.

His eyes feasted on the unblemished flesh as familiar stirrings woke beneath. 'Oooh-weee! Ya c'd drive a man mad!'

A figure moved beyond the office windows.

The desk clerk snapped the magazine shut and froze. He'd turned off the sign half an hour ago. There shouldn't be anyone coming here tonight.

Then the figure moved again, and he caught the pale outline of a woman's dress. That weird old biddy!

A wicked thought sparked in his mind. His bristles spread in a broad grin. He glanced down.

Shame to waste a grade A piece of excitement like that on a paper female.

Loosening his robe, he rushed to the door and jerked it open.

'Aunt Hortense' was halfway across the central lawn, aiming uncertainty for a flowerbed.

'Give us a look, sweetie!' boomed the desk clerk.

'C'mon, honeybunch – show us those big blue eyes!'

And, as Clyde turned, he whipped open his robe, thrusting forward his bare and bony thighs, with a cackle of joy.

Clyde gibbered in delight. After a grindingly boring day this evening was turning out quite playful.

Flashing his teeth, he snatched at the hem of his dress and yanked it up to his chin.

The desk clerk's cackle dried instantly. His eyes bugged. Wrapping his robe on his deflating manhood, he leapt back into the office, slamming the door and sliding the bolt. He slumped against the wall, gasping for breath.

'Holy Jesus ...' he mouthed.

It was obvious the moment Philo opened the office door, just after nine the following morning, that 'Aunt Hortense's' secret was out.

'I told ya the rules!' the desk clerk bellowed. 'No pets includes apes too!'

'Yeah, well I'm sorry,' Philo conceded. 'But there's no harm done.'

He dropped the chalet keys on the desk and turned to go. He really had too much else on his mind to take up petty arguments.

But the clerk thought differently. 'No harm!' he snapped, pop eyes popping even further. 'He's a menace! Goes round peekin' in windows! Ogled at me last night while I was gettin' it on with two young beauties!'

Philo gave him a doubtful look. The man might have shaved this morning but he still had the visual appeal of the average barn door.

'Look,' Philo snapped, 'Clyde has no interest in human sex. What were you doin'? Gettin' it on with a couple o' apes?'

The desk clerk exploded. 'Get out! Out!' he roared.

Philo obliged.

There was a large, ruby-coloured Pontiac parked to one side of the office. Jack Wilson was leaning against the bonnet, dressed in slacks and an open necked shirt, with his arms folded, waiting patiently.

Philo looked at him in surprise.

'Let's go,' said the other abruptly. He straightened up and made for the driver's door.

'The fight ain't on till noon,' said Philo.

Wilson paused, his look measuring Philo. 'Yeah, I know that. But I found out where they're holdin' Lynne – an' the best time t' hit 'em is when they move 'er.' The two men stared at each other as the realisation slowly dawned on Philo that his friendship had not been misplaced. His grin surfaced at the same moment, combining gratitude with a tacit apology for his attitude of the previous day. Wilson returned it.

Philo jumped for the front passenger seat, just as Orville ambled across the lawn with Clyde in tow.

'What's goin' on?' he asked.

Philo snatched open the car door. 'He found out where Lynne is.'

'Let's go!' cried Orville eagerly.

'Uh – 'Wilson paused, halfway into the car. He glanced quickly at Philo. 'No. They're packin' heat an' they might use it.'

'I'm 'is friend an' Clyde's 'is friend,' said Orville emphatically. 'We go.' And he made straight for the rear door.

Philo shrugged and slid into the front beside Wilson.

'Hop in there, kid,' Orville ordered, ushering Clyde into the back.

The engine fired and the car swung in a tight circle. They drove in silence through the centre of Jackson and took the turning to Jackson Hole and the Grand Teton National Park.

Eventually Wilson looked across at Philo.

'I had a few words with Mr Patrick Scarfe last night,' he explained. 'He wasn't too happy you and I'd been talkin'.' Philo acknowledged this with a wry smile. 'But I wheedled it out of 'im.'

'I'm obliged,' said Philo. 'Do we know how many are holdin' 'er?'

Wilson blipped the accelerator as the road ahead cleared. 'Four o' them,' he said. 'They're friends of Scarfe, so they won't be playin' around.'

Philo stroked the side of his head nostalgically. He had several scores to settle

'We met,' he said.

Wilson nodded. 'Then I suggest one of us grabs Lynne straight out and gets her clear. That'll leave two of us with a clear field.'

Orville raised a hand in the rear mirror. 'I'll do the grabbin'.' He grinned. 'Hell, either o' you two could flatten the average platoon. I'd only be window dressin'.'

'OK by me,' said Wilson.

The last cluster of town houses passed behind them.

A motel sign loomed ahead.

'This is it,' he said.

They turned into a narrow curving driveway. The motel was a long low chalet-style building at the top with a discreet hedge in front of it as high as a car roof. Not until the driveway curved past the hedge did Philo see the familiar long black Cadillac. It was parked at the end of a row of four cars.

There seemed to be no one around.

Wilson slowed the Pontiac to a crawl, negotiated the small forecourt directly below the building and slotted in beside the Caddie.

He turned to Philo and pointed meaningfully at the door directly in front of them. The windows on either side were still curtained.

Philo nodded and twisted to the back of the car. He reached across to Clyde and pressed a finger to his lips.

'Keep ya head down, ol' buddy, and not a word.'

The orang-utan grunted and slipped down between the seats. All three men eased open the car doors and climbed out. Philo motioned towards the corner of the building, a few yards to their right. Eyes fixed on the motel door, they scurried silently round the corner, flattening themselves against the clapboard wall.

'How long?' whispered Philo.

Wilson shrugged. 'Not too long. They'll drive 'er around till noon. Less chance of being disturbed that way.'

Orville, his head closest to the corner, gave a loud hiss.

The door to Lynne's room was opening.

There was a pause while all three men tensed. Then the tallest of Beekman's heavies stepped out under the awning, his gaze sweeping up and down the line of cars, his hand conspicuously in the jacket of his grey check suit. Orville ducked back behind the corner.

Satisfied, the heavy turned back to the open door and nodded.

Lynne emerged between two of the other men. She

looked pale and tired, but otherwise unhurt. The leader, Dino, brought up the rear, turning to close the door behind him.

Orville glanced at Philo, then reversed his peaked cap. Philo patted his shoulder.

As the first three heavies drew level with the front of the Cadillac Orville sucked in a deep breath and ran. The small hunched figure, bursting out of nowhere, took the gunmen by surprise. Lynne shrieked as Orville's outstretched arm clutched her round the waist, lifting her bodily off the ground. Then both of them were rolling over the grass beside the Caddie.

As the tallest heavy gaped at them, Philo leapt out and sank a fist into his gut. He doubled over with a grunt, in time to catch a vicious upper cut that slapped his head to the right.

Meanwhile, Wilson buffaloed straight into Lynne's two flanking guards, seizing them both under the throat and pitching them backwards onto the Cadillac's bonnet by sheer momentum.

Only Dino was left untouched. He snapped a hand under his armpit and drew out his Colt, aiming it directly at Philo's head as the other stepped back from his moaning opponent.

Struggling up from the ground, Orville saw him.

'Hey!' he yelled, appalled.

Unthinking, Dino switched his aim and squeezed the trigger. As the gun exploded, Wilson knocked the man's extended arm upwards and kicked him sideways.

Orville felt a jolt under his left shoulder and stumbled back in surprise. As Lynne gasped, he saw blood bubble through a tear in his tee-shirt.

The fight rapidly became a free for all, with the odds stacked high against the heavies. Philo went to help out Wilson with the two heavies and Dino. Flooring one, he found himself attacked from behind by the grey-suited man he'd already flattened once. Philo deflected a jab to his kidney and clubbed the heavy on the neck. He grunted and lurched to one side. Philo let loose a barrage of sharp jabs to the chest and gut. As the man folded, his arms swinging wildly, Philo elbowed him in the chest and clutched at his jacket lapels.

The man found himself tumbling across the Caddie's bonnet; he crashed, winded, on the ground next to Wilson's Pontiac.

From his vantage point in the front pasenger seat, Clyde blinked down at him curiously through the open window.

Wilson, meanwhile, was smoothly demolishing Dino. He had the smaller man against the motel wall, his arms spread wide and his mouth gasping as he vainly tried to fend off a storm of shattering blows.

Philo was busy holding another heavy upright, raining punches on his lolling chin, when he saw the danger. The grey-suited man was rising from beside the Pontiac. His lip trickled blood and he moved unsteadily, but the automatic in his hands was rock steady. Its muzzle pointed straight at Wilson's back.

Philo let his man drop with a thump.

'Right turn, Clyde!' he cried.

The hairy fist shot from the car window. It struck the heavy's jaw with a crack that even made Philo wince. Glassy-eyed, the heavy bumped against the Cadillac, his gun slipping from his fingers.

Wilson turned round in time to see the man fall. Behind him, an exhausted Dino slid to the ground.

The fight was over.

As Wilson snatched up the guns, stuffing them into his belt, Philo turned to Lynne. She was kneeling on the grass, next to a pale and incredulous Orville.

'You all right?' Philo asked her.

'I'm fine,' she gasped, and went back to Orville's wound.

Philo glanced at him, frowning.

'Why don't you get the cops and an ambulance?' he said to Wilson.

Wilson was hauling the grey-suited man back onto his feet. He propped him against the Cadillac's bonnet, next to Dino. 'Now the cops ain't part of the bargain,' he warned.

Philo looked at him.

'All right – just the ambulance then.'

Wilson nodded and bent to drag Philo's victims off the ground.

Philo caught Orville's gaze. 'That bullet was mine,' he said.

Orville's clown face folded into a foolish grin.

'Well, I like bein' a hero too sometimes, you know,' he said.

Philo didn't return the grin. He would happily take anything the heaviest heavies threw at him but when they endangered his nearest and dearest he found it increasingly hard to accept it gracefully. 'Well, you're doin' a good job with it,' he told Orville, and meant it.

Orville reddened and grinned all the more.

Wilson, meanwhile, had assembled Beekman's battered troops.

'Now look,' he snarled, thrusting Dino's automatic under its owner's nose,' I just saved you guys' ass from the slam - so now they belong t' me. An' if I ever see ya again, I'm gonna come an' collect 'em. So you just get in this car an' you just keep drivin' west till you see the surf. Got it? *Move!*'

He jerked open the Cadillac's front passenger door and thrust Dino inside. The others needed no prompting. As the car started up, reversed and squealed away at speed, Wilson turned to Philo and raised his eyebrows. Philo nodded with a faint smile.

'I owe ya one,' he said as they followed the wailing ambulance back into town.

'Uh-huh.' Wilson shook his head. He took his hand off the steering wheel to indicate the back of the car. 'We're even. Your hairy friend there saved my skin for me.'

In the back seat Lynne ruffled Clyde's scalp. He whistled softly.

'We're even then,' Philo agreed.

His gaze lifted, catching Lynne's in the rear mirror. In only these few short days of absence he had forgotten how very good she could look. He could stop the car right now and start exploring her all over again. Her momentary look of softness seemed to read, and match his thoughts, but her words pushed his mind in a direction he'd almost forgotten.

'You're not gonna fight, are ya?' she asked.

Philo hesitated. He glanced out the side window. So far all he had was his word against Beekman's threats and promises. But judging by the look of Jackson the whole enterprise had its own momentum by now.

'Well,' he concluded, 'if I don't it's a forfeit. A lot o' people bet money on me an' not all of 'em're rich.'

Wilson drew a deep breath.

'Well, if neither one of us showed up, then there wouldn't be any fight.' He turned to Philo. 'Then all the bets'd be off.'

Philo spotted Lynne's broad reflected smile, and grinned.

'That's somethin' t' think about,' he agreed.

'Wilson!'

In his hotel suite James Beekman gazed in angry disbelief at the telephone in his hand. He turned to Patrick Scarfe. 'He hung up!' He slammed the receiver down in disgust. 'Well, that's it,' he snapped, stalking away. 'Neither of them're gonna show.'

Scarfe's expression was one of unalloyed relief. 'All the bets're off then!'

His employer was a man who could stretch an odd further than any human being he'd ever met, and always come out smelling of roses, but the thought of a million dollar wager with a top Mafia Don had given Scarfe a sleepless night.

'Damn it!' roared Beekham. 'I spent a lot o' time, a lot o' money settin' this thing up!'

He paused and Scarfe waited for Beekman's unfailing sense of equilibrium to reassert itself. It might not be an inappropriate moment to remind him of the few pounds he'd lost in sweat during Anthony Paoli's visit.

Beekman let go a long sigh.

'Well – ' He shrugged, then gestured vaguely at the phone. 'I think you better let the sporting folks know.'

'Yeah,' agreed Scarfe, and, beaming, dived straight for the receiver.

At the local hospital Orville's 'hunting accident' turned out to be little more than a flesh wound. Dino's bullet had passed straight through, missing the bone and causing minimal muscle damage. Growing perkier by the minute, Orville was cleaned up, bandaged and given a couple of shots for shock before being carted upstairs for a period of routine observation.

His room was cool and bright with a glimpse of mountains through the white shaded windows.

He sat up in bed with his arm in a sling. Philo and Lynne were alone with him, while Wilson looked after Clyde in the parking lot below.

'So,' Orville asked. 'Are you gonna fight?'

Deliberately, Philo did not look at Lynne as he answered. Now that both Orville and Lynne were safe he found his options opening up again. Wilson was still outside – and unbeaten; still the toughest, most challenging opponent Philo had ever faced. But he couldn't expect Lynne to see it that way.

'I don't know,' he said, awkwardly. 'That depends on Wilson.' Then he did look at Lynne. 'You wanna stay here with Orville?'

She nodded, reaching across to Orville's good arm, though her gaze was far from certain.

Philo turned for the door.

'Oh, say!' Orville flashed a bright grin. 'On your way out could you kind o' tell the nurses what a hero I am?'

Philo smiled wryly. He'd already caught his friend entertaining one attractive nurse with a highly embellished account of this morning's events on his way out the treatment room.

'Now, why didn't I think o' that?' he said.

Lynne was laughing.

Philo pushed open the door and two nurses tripped from the corridor outside. One was small and dark, the other bosomy and blonde with a peaches and cream smile under a neat fringe – just Orville's style.

'Is that the hero?' the blonde asked breathlessly.

'Oh yeah,' Philo confirmed. 'That's him lying right there.'

134

The nurses brushed past him and hurried to Orville's bedside.

'You're a good man, Philo Beddoe!' he yelled after Philo's retreating back.

The blonde's cool fingers adjusted his sling.

'Oh,' he murmured, sinking back on his pillow. 'It hurts right here.'

In the parking lot Jack Wilson was leaning against the side of his Pontiac, feeding Clyde through the open window with bananas he'd begged from the hospital kitchen.

He looked up with a smile as Philo approached. 'The young man's gotta real healthy appetite.'

Philo grinned, 'That he does.'

Wilson let Clyde handle the last banana for himself. Then he straightened up. From the look in his eyes it was clear to Philo that the other man had been having much the same thoughts as himself.

Wilson sucked in breath. 'I don't think we c'n end it even,' he said carefully. Philo nodded. They weren't going to argue on this point.

'I don't think,' he said.

Wilson sniffed. 'But then on the other hand, I don't have any great desire t' make Beekman rich.'

The assumption of victory made Philo chuckle. 'You figure you would?' he asked.

Wilson nodded.

'Figure.' He paused. 'But then I guess we'll just t' find out if I would've or not huh?'

Slowly the two bareknuckle champions began to smile at each other.

For Philo the moment was as sudden and certain as his decision to quit. Quit he would - whether as basket case or unbeaten victor - but this battle of giants was as inevitable as the sun peeping over the San Gabriels every California morning.

He nodded slowly. 'I guess,' he said.

CHAPTER 14

Gloom enshrouded Fat Zack's Snow King suite. Patrick Scarfe's phone call had dashed the party's buoyant spirits as swiftly and as surely as a plunge into a mountain stream. They sprawled about the main room, gazing gloomily into space. Even Zack's cigar had gone out.

'Real shame ...' he declared mournfully.

'It would've been the fight of the century,' commented Little Melvin.

Long John nodded slowly. 'Sure as hell would've.'

Candy, curled at Long John's feet, gave a long, heartfelt sigh, an effort that caused her bosom to bulge alarmingly in the tight, low-cut top she wore. To her mild surprise Long John did not so much as flicker an eyelid.

Downstairs in the forecourt two sober-suited businessmen tossed their luggage in the back of a taxi to take them to the airport and a waiting executive jet. Unlike their arrival the previous day, their faces matched their suits.

'Just blew a hundred thousand dollar deal t' get out here for this fight!' complained one.

'Well, hell,' the other agreed, 'it'd've been worth it.'

Several blocks away the chef and two lingering guests contemplated the rows of empty tables in the Jackson Hole Bar-B-Q's balcony restaurant.

'Wilson would've taken 'im,' concluded the guest in the check shirt.

His tall young companion grunted scornfully. 'The hell he would have.'

The chef threw a soiled dishcloth on the table in disgust.

'Who cares?' he snapped and stalked away.

He'd lost six burgers the previous morning by rushing to glimpse Philo and Wilson on the street. Not to mention the two hundred dollars he'd have made on a Philo victory.

Oblivious to the consternation they had caused, Philo and Wilson toured the back lots of Jackson, searching for a suitable venue. It needed to be roomy and quiet and as private as they could make it; at this moment their contest concerned only themselves.

A block behind the tourist shops and the smart restaurants Jackson became homely and countrified: stockpens and woodpiles, clapboard houses and well-weathered barns. It was one of the latter that Philo indicated with a quick nod of his head. Wilson grunted agreement and pulled over onto a strip of wheel-rutted grass. They stepped out. The barn stood in a quiet corner with rusting pieces of agricultural equipment stacked on either side. It had an air of slightly picturesque neglect, its boards rimed with lichen, a sign announcing 'Jackson Feed' in brown flaking letters facing them.

Philo reached back into the car for Clyde who swung down to the ground, grabbing his hand.

Wilson moved across the grass to a small window in the facing wall and rubbed dust away from the glass. After peering inside, he turned to Philo and then tried a door to one side. A metal pin hanging by a piece of twine was all that held the latch shut.

Philo and Clyde followed Wilson inside, closing the door behind them.

It was dim and dusty, ripe with the musty odour of old straw which littered the floor. Golden shafts of sunlight picked out a dozen fresh bales piled at one end, a waist-high loading platform at the other, and in between dark supporting posts for the floor above.

It was hardly an impressive venue for any normal national championship, but perfect for these contestants.

Philo drew Clyde towards the new bales of hay.

'Get up there,' he ordered. Gibbering acknowledgement, the great ape leapt up onto the bundles and settled himself, sniffing curiously at the strange material.

At the farther end of the barn Wilson was shrugging off his shirt. He wore a bright blue vest underneath, its hem hanging down over his slacks.

Philo glanced down at his tee-shirt. He'd leave it on today.

He had a feeling even the thinnest layer of cotton – feeble as it was for protection – shouldn't be neglected in this bout.

He'd already changed into his training shoes for a last session of jogging this morning.

He glanced at Wilson through the brilliant sun shafts. They looked like misplaced spotlights, vainly searching out the participants in the great event.

Both men took deep breaths. They were ready.

The three boys were aged eight, nine and ten, the last two being brothers, which made it doubly difficult for the girl, who was not only their sister but aged only eight.

'Wait for me!' she wailed, her short legs pounding the dust as she pursued them across the empty back lot.

'She's catching up!' hissed the nine-year-old, casting a look over his shoulder.

The eight-year-old giggled.

'I heard that!' the girl shouted.

The boys slid between two sheds and across a narrow shadowed yard towards the back of a large barn.

The ten-year-old rounded its corner first, then caught a movement through a dust-smeared window. He skidded to a halt, so that the two brothers cannoned into him, and stared through the glass, shading his eyes. Inside a sharp right to the jaw from Philo sent Wilson stumbling back across the floor.

'Hey, look at this!' the ten-year-old yelled.

'What? What?' the others cried, jostling to see.

'Wow!' exclaimed the eight-year-old, glimpsing Wilson's ferocious return: a sharp series of jabs to Philo's gut. This was better than TV.

Behind the boys the girl had arrived and started jumping up and down, pulling at their backs.

138

'Let me see!! Let me see!' she called.

So great was their excitement none of them noticed the police patrol car glide to a halt beside Wilson's Pontiac. Over the crackle of his radio, the young officer in the passenger seat called through his open window:

'All right you kids, what're you doin' here?'

Ignoring him, all four shrieked as Philo slipped a jarring upper cut under Wilson's guard.

Sighing, the officer climbed out of the car.

'I said, what're you kids doin' here?' he snapped.

The girl turned and saw him for the first time. She tugged at her younger brother's arm, but he took no notice.

'C'monnn, move back,' the officer continued boredly. He began to push them away from the window.

'Move back!'

Groaning, the three boys shifted reluctantly. The officer shooed them away toward the pavement. Then he bowed to the glass.

Reeling under a rain of Wilson's blows, Philo ducked back into a pillar of sunlight.

The officer tensed, his eyes widening. He rubbed the glass, peering closer. Wilson jumped sideways into the same beam as Philo met his attack.

The officer swallowed. He'd seen both contestants in town yesterday. There was no mistake.

His mouth opened. He gabbled, 'It's ... it's on ... it's ...' Back in the car his companion looked up in surprise as the officer flung open the door and gestured wildly at the radio. 'The fight ...' he cried. 'Gimme that!'

'What?' the second officer frowned.

But the first snatched at the radio mike, jerking it away from the dash and thumbing the transmit bar.

'Jackson base. Jackson base,' he snapped. 'This is car two. The fight - the fight is on. Here!'

Five miles to the south a disgruntled trucker, two days out on a tight schedule because of his detour through Jackson, hunched over the wheel of his giant rig, his CB switched to the local police frequency. The young officer's message burst through in a gabble of sound. Then the meaning became clear.

The trucker's eyes brightened, his shoulders lifted. Reaching forward he thumbed the selector for channel nineteen – calling channel for all truckers and CB enthusiasts in the immediate vicinity.

He picked up his microphone. 'Breaker, breaker one-nine,' he called. 'There's a good news channel ...'

Two miles down the road Philo's spinsterly fans, the one still in pink and her sister resolutely white, leaned forward in the back seat of their Cadillac.

'It's on!' the trucker's voice boomed from the CB set. 'The fight is on!'

The lady in white turned breathlessly to her sister. 'Did you hear that? Oh!' She clapped her lace gloved hands together in joy.

Her sister reached forward and poked their young chauffeur firmly in the back. 'Well?' she snapped. 'Whatcha waitin' for, *dummy*!' The sisters chuckled together, then burst into shrill giggles, as the Cadillac instantly swung across the highway in a tyre-squealing U-turn.

The word was spreading.

In his suite on the third floor of the Ramada Snow King James Beekman was tucking into an early lunch. He would be flying out in half an hour in time to catch his New York connection at Cheyenne and the prospect of airline food did not enthrall him. He had accepted the day's disasters grudgingly but philosophically. All he wanted now was to move on as soon as possible.

'Aren'tcha gonna have any?' he asked Partick Scarfe, lifting his fork with half a tomato stuck on the end. 'Here!'

Scarfe shook his head in mild disgust. He had just spent a blistering five minutes on the phone with Dino. And his employer's eating habits had never impressed him.

The telephone rang.

His mouth full, Beekman gestured toward Scarfe to answer it. 'Yeah?' The other spoke dully into the receiver. His second 'Yeah!' sounded a lot more involved. His face was alive as he slammed the receiver down. 'Jim!' he cried.

Beekman grunted 'Huh?' through a half chewed lettuce leaf.

'The fight is on!' Scarfe cried. 'The fight!'

Swallowing hard, Beekman threw down his fork. 'What time is it?'

Scarfe groped for his wristwatch. 'Uuuuu – it's eleven-fifty.'

His employer shot to his feet.

'Well, all bets don't cancel till noon,' he said, reaching for his jacket. 'That means all bets are still on.'

Struggling into the jacket, he made for the door.

'C'mon, let's go! Let's go!' he snapped.

At about the same moment the news reached the Jackson airport terminal building. Orderly files of passengers broke immediately; private owners already in their aircraft quickly cancelled flight plans; tussles developed at the cab ranks.

Fat Zack's executive jet was approaching the end of the runway and turning into the wind when Sweet Sue answered a call from the tower.

Her mouth formed a perfect circle; she stared at Zack. 'It's on!' she shrieked.

Zack gaped at her over his cigar. 'What!'

'The fight!' screamed the blonde.

As the members of his party hooted happily behind him, Zack glanced out the side of the cockpit. There was a wide open gate in the perimeter fence only a few dozen yards from the jet. Beyond it was the road to Jackson. Without a second's hesitation Zack kicked the rudder bar over. Slowly, majestically, its twin engines whining, the jet taxied off the runway, through the gateway and headed into town.

The chef of the Jackson Hole Bar-B-Q looked up from four

half cooked burgers and listened. Shouts and cries and the sounds of running feet were filtering up from the street. It sounded like a riot.

Frowning, he stepped out onto the balcony restaurant. The tables were deserted.

He moved to the parapet. Men were running down the street, shouting and laughing. One looked up and caught sight of the chef.

'It's on!' the runner yelled. 'The fight's on!'

The chef stared at him in surprise. Then he smiled, flung down his white cap and dashed for the stairs. A thin wisp of black smoke curled out the kitchen door.

For once the Black Widows' outrageous head gear was attracting no attention. Swept on by an eager and oblivious crowd, they trotted in a body down Jackson's main street, led by Cholla, riding crop in hand.

'Hey, Cholla,' queried Elmo, 'what're we doin' on foot?' His pained expression, shared by the rest of the Widows, showed how uneasy he felt without two-wheeled transport. A biker without a chopper was really no different from any other shmuck.

Cholla sighed, equally peeved. He'd had a bad morning dodging questions when the Widows had risen at their campsite to find themselves bikeless.

'I told ya,' he snapped, 'The cops pinched the bikes!'

Elmo considered this.

'Yeah, but what for?' he asked.

Cholla lashed sideways with his crop.

'Who fills this outfit anyway, you or me?' he snarled.

Dutifully Elmo fell back in line.

The crowd outside the old barn was over a hundred deep and growing fast. They jostled to see through the few small windows, they scuffled inside the open door, they shouted and groaned and screamed encouragement and abuse. And inside, ignoring it all, Philo and Wilson fought the fight of their professional lives.

Sweat already coated them both, yet neither showed any serious mark.

There was no professional trick, Philo had quickly realised, that Wilson didn't know. Every feint, every block, every parry that would have floored hundreds of less competent fighters, Wilson could match when he didn't foresee it. Philo had to be clever and fast and after all the tricky work, all the technique he still had to beat down the sheer bull-like strength of the man. He had never worked so hard in a fight before.

Wilson came in low with a series of teeth-jarring hammer blows to Philo's gut. Taking them, Philo rationed his breath, then Wilson over-reached and Philo saw his opening. He dived in with a vicious left to the stomach, catching his opponent unprepared.

As Wilson gasped, Philo tried for an upper cut and connected. It was a merciless blow, lifting the man onto his toes as he hurtled backwards into the wall of the barn. The boards were old already and no match for two hundred and twenty flying pounds.

A whole section of the wall exploded outwards. The crowd shrieked and jostled back as Wilson crashed among them in a shower of broken boards.

Philo was instantly behind him, looking for the follow up. But Wilson was on his feet, slicing back. Swapping blows, they battled across the grass and onto the roadway, spectators milling about them.

Ignored by the multitude Clyde picked his way carefully through the gap in the wall and rolled in pursuit.

Fortunately for Zack the streets of Jackson were wide and relatively uncluttered by telephone and power lines. At a gentle five miles an hour he taxied down the main street while excited pedestrians trotted under the wing tips on either side. He could have gone a lot faster but he saw no necessity to earn himself a speeding ticket. At the end of the next block the crowd showed signs of thickening.

Zack throttled back still further. 'We'll run around the corner and we'll be ringside, boys!' he announced.

The jet halted at the intersection. The street beyond was packed. From the cockpit Philo and Wilson were plainly visible, slogging it out in a tight circle in the crowd.

Zack hurried out of his seat, opened the exit hatch and led the way down onto the road.

Laughing and giggling, his party followed him.

'C'mon, Zack,' Long John cried, clutching Candy's hand and making for the crowd. 'Let's go, boys!'

Zack grabbed at Sweet Sue. He couldn't remember having so much excitement since his daddy had given him his first oil well for Christmas. Sweet Sue giggled and clicked after him on high, unsteady heels. She'd never seen a town go so wild. Then she glimpsed what looked like a hairy ape bowling out of a side turning. She blinked and looked again. It was still coming. She giggled even louder. This town was *really* wild.

'Clyde!' hissed Orville.

The great ape's head swung round at the familiar voice, and gibbered in happy recognition. He'd completely lost sight of Philo and all this mad rushing about was beginning to bother him. It was worse than a zoo.

He slipped his hand gratefully into Orville's.

'Friend o' mine,' said the other, grinning bashfully at his newly acquired girlfriend. The blonde nurse with the peaches and cream look smiled back at him. She'd already decided Orville was a kook when he'd leapt out of bed the instant news of the fight hit the hospital. The orang-utan did not seem out of character.

'Quick!' urged Lynne, pushing on into the crowd.

All three reached the edge of the fight as Philo and Wilson sparred in mid-street, next to a row of parked cars.

Both were red-faced and grunting. A risky side swipe from Wilson went awry and Philo leapt into the opening with sharp jabs to the heart.

'That's it! That's it!' Orville cried

'C'mon, baby!' screamed a spinsterly lady in pink who stood beside him. 'C'mon – we have a pot full on ya!'

'C'mon, baby!' echoed a twin in white at her side. Caught off balance, Wilson tottered back, vainly trying to fend off Philo's attack. There were bruises on his cheeks and his eyes became suddenly desperate. Then he was against a parked car, sprawling back over the bonnet as Philo's punches developed a maniacal ferocity.

'Come on Philo!' yelled an excited Long John, across the ring.

Next to him Beekman and Scarfe looked on, appalled. 'C'mon!' C'mon!' Beekman urged Wilson.

Beekman was sweating almost as much as the fighter. He dabbed nervously at his cheek with a handkerchief. But Wilson's defensive efforts were slowing; his head lolled against the car bonnet. Triumph flared in Philo's eyes. Beekman panicked. He clutched at Scarfe's arm.

'Kill 'im,' he hissed.

Scarfe gaped at him, incredulous.

'You heard me!' Beekman snarled. 'Right now!'

Swallowing, Scarfe looked round quickly. He'd seen Dino and his men only a few seconds ago. Then he spotted them, high on a balcony behind the parked cars, gazing down at the fight. They were perfectly placed.

Rising on his toes he waved desperately. Dino caught sight of him and cocked his head questioningly. Scarfe made the shape of a gun with his fingers and jabbed them twice at Philo.

Dino nodded, a thin smile crossing his bruised face.

His hand moved inside his jacket.

But the pantomime had not gone unnoticed.

On the opposite side of the makeshift ring, jostled repeatedly by his enthusiastic followers, Cholla watched with a growing frown.

On the balcony Dino drew a gun, holding it down in front of him below the balcony rail. He reached into a side pocket and withdrew the long black cylinder of a silencer.

Cholla spun to the Widows.

'Hey, listen! Listen up!' He jerked a thumb behind him. 'That's Beekman's hoods up there! They're gonna kill Beddoe!'

Elmo beamed. 'Hey, Cholla, that's great! Let's give 'em a hand!'

'You twit!' Cholla roared at him. 'I sold all the bikes and put every nickle we had on Beddoe t' win!'

Elmo's face dropped. 'Cholla, how could you?'

Discontent growled among the Widows behind him.

'We've been at war with Beddoe for over a year! complained Dallas.

'Listen!' Cholla gestured the bikers to huddle in a circle, their heads down. 'War is war,' he hissed, 'but *business* is *business*. If Beddoe loses we are flat *busted*!'

There was a pause while they considered this.

'Hell, yeah!' said Dallas suddenly. 'Business is business!'

'So don't just stand their, you frepts!' Cholla cried, breaking the circle. 'Go get 'em!'

As one, yelling and screaming with a blood lust that had had precious few outlets in the previous weeks, the Widows stampeded toward the balcony stairs.

Dino was levelling his silencer on the balcony rail and drawing a bead on Philo's bobbing back when he glimpsed a sudden movement out of the side of his eye. Glancing sideways, he saw what looked like an ill dressed golliwog with a bright orange mop bursting out of the stairwell. He blinked in disbelief. In that split second Elmo's punch flattened his nose against his cheek. The gun spun into the crowd.

The Widows spilled onto the balcony, driving back the four heavies.

The tall one in grey aimed a punch at Elmo who ducked. The heavy's fist grazed his scalp and he made a sudden grab. The hair came away in his hand. He gasped in shock and Elmo cackled loudly. Dallas took the opportunity to flatten him.

Outnumbered by almost three to one, Beekman's troops fared little better than in their earlier battle of the day. Cholla – ever aware of the need to protect the centre of command – hung back at the top of the stairs, observing the battle with an air of gleeful detachment.

In a few hectic moments two of the enemy slumped unconscious against the wall and another was pitched unceremoniously over the balcony rail. Screaming, he crashed through the windshield of a parked car, his legs jutting bizarrely across the bonnet. The last lurched

146

toward the stairwell, Cholla obligingly making room for him. Glassy-eyed, he teetered on the top stair. With a chuckle, Cholla lowered his riding crop and gently goosed the man from behind. With a high-pitched squeak he tumbled down the stairs. Breathless but victorious, the Widows beamed at each other.

In the street below, Wilson's sudden leap from the bonnet where he had been pinned staved off imminent defeat. In a desperate urge to finish it then and there Philo had expended more energy than he'd realised. He was panting now as Wilson punched his way to a recovery. Philo took the blows, searching for his opening. It came and Philo sliced; he caught the side of Wilson's head and the fighter reeled backwards across the sidewalk, crashing into a balcony post.

Gasping, Philo pressed forward. But Wilson raised a hand.

Slowly he sank onto the edge of the sidewalk.

Taking a deep breath, Philo lowered his fists.

They were both close to exhaustion, bruised and battered with their vests in tatters, speckled with blood from cracked lips and split cheeks.

Philo coughed and sank down next to his opponent.

Around them the crowd grew quiet.

Philo's spinsterly fan in pink handed him a can of soft drink. He swigged and offered it to Wilson.

'We c'n end it here, you know,' Philo said between gasps.

Wilson turned his head to him. 'Even?'

Philo shook his head slowly. It was still an effort to speak. 'No,' he said. 'You owe me one.'

Candy pushed her way to the front of the crowd where Sweet Sue was already standing.

Both the fighters looked beat.

'Hey,' asked the redhead, 'is it over?'

Sweet Sue shrugged. 'I don't know.'

Murmurs began to trickle through the crowd.

Wilson handed the drink can back to its donor. There was a ghost of a smile about his swollen lips.

147

'Think I'd buy that – while I'm still standin'?' he rasped.

Philo looked at him. 'Nope,' he said.

Wearily, they dragged themselves to their feet.

The crowd burst into wild applause.

The restaurant was one of Jackson's smartest, specialising in a thoughtful mixture of Italian cuisine and the contents of the area's mountain lakes and streams. Prices were high and behind its neat red and white striped awning few at the crowded tables within were willing to forego the pleasures of an expensive menu simply to satisfy their curiosity about the racket in the street. Which made it doubly galling when both the awning and the plate glass window below it suddenly burst in upon them, and an oblivious Philo and Wilson crashed after the debris, scattering tables, chairs, plates and diners on every side with equal abandon.

Cries of protest and alarm were drowned almost instantly in the roar of the crowd which pressed through the gaping hole in the shopfront, stepping over debris and diners alike as Philo and Wilson fought their way across the restaurant. A tall, smart-suited man rose from his side table, wine glass in hand, gaping in amazement as the carnival passed him.

Flanked by his bodyguards, Anthony Paoli Senior negotiated the tables. As he drew level with the standing diner, he lifted the wine glass from the man's hand, sipped at it appreciatively and moved on. The diner did not notice it go. From the kitchens two wide-eyed chefs watched the brawling men approach them. In sudden panic they realised Philo and Wilson could exit no other way. Clutching their white caps they hared for the exit as Philo, reeling under a vicious sideswipe from Wilson, cannoned through the swing doors, clutching at worktops and side cupboards to stop himself falling. Pots and pans clattered to the floor yet he only partially succeeded.

He crashed on one knee against a range, his right arm outstretched against the warm black metal.

Wilson was directly behind him, poised for a final blow. But the outstretched arm was too obvious a target.

Gasping, he lashed out with his foot, catching the arm just below the elbow.

There was an audible crack.

Philo's face went white; his head lopped forward, dripping sweat.

Wilson hesitated, staring at him, only slowly realising what he had done.

He stabbed a finger at Philo.

'It's broke!' he cried. 'That's it!'

Philo's head rose; his teeth were a white line, his face muscles clenched in rigid lines of pain. 'No, it ain't,' he growled.

Wilson's growing expression of triumph froze and became serious. He stared at Philo, then gestured emphatically. 'That's *it*,' he said.

Behind him Fat Zack forced his way through the mob jostling at the doorway. He took one look at Philo's twisted limb and yelled back into the packed restaurant: 'His arm's broke!'

The news spread like wildfire. Hushed whispers, then cries of protest, disbelief, despair.

Lynne pushed past the plump Texan with Orville and Clyde close behind.

She rushed over to Philo who was nursing his shattered forearm. She gasped as she saw it, her eyes close to tears. 'Stop this,' she cried. 'It doesn't matter.'

Philo's face was a mask of pain. 'It matters t' me,' he hissed.

Lynne turned despairing eyes on Wilson. He strode up and down, all too aware of the ways his last two bouts had ended. He was a professional fighter, not a maimer, a killer; he'd had enough accidents to last a lifetime.

'Beddoe,' he snapped, stopping. 'We're even.'

Gasping, Philo rose awkwardly to his feet, bracing himself against the range. His arm hung limply; his head leaned to one side. He looked a wreck.

Appalled, Wilson and Lynne, Orville and Clyde watched him.

'I owe ya,' he rasped

When the blow came Wilson did not believe it until its sledgehammer force spun him round and sent him lurching through the exit door, ripping the plywood off its hinges. Turning, he found Philo on him. He lunged crabwise, shielding his dangling arm and punching hard and accurately with his left. Wilson's disbelief lasted only a second. Then he was fighting for his life.

Led by Lynne and Orville the crowd spilled after them through the restaurant kitchen.

'C'mon,' snapped Orville, dragging a momentarily distracted Clyde. 'Put that spaghetti down! C'mon!'

Still parrying, Wilson moved back across the sidewalk and through the entrance to a small park, under a decorative archway of bleached steerhorns, twisted together like a gigantic crown of thorns.

Philo was no longer a man; he was a blind, insensate force, a driving self-destructive machine which simply didn't know the meaning of rest or pain or defeat.

For the first time Wilson felt fear, not the kind of fear he could twist into hate and anger and turn to his own advantage; this was closer to awe, a kind of helpless incomprehension.

He could feel his foundations shifting. Then his foot slipped on the grass.

It was all Philo needed. His punches came straight from the shoulder: fast, sure and vicious, each one enough to floor a lesser man. Three times he connected squarely with Wilson's jaw. Reeling back, the man cried out in pain.

Then he was on his knees, panting like a wounded bull, struggling forward, his eyes staring in horror and sheer disbelief at defeat, the one fact he'd never known before. Philo's fourth blow was an uppercut. It started below his waist, met the centre of Wilson's jaw and snapped it hard against his skull. As the swing continued upwards, Wilson rolled over and back, crashing onto the grass.

Spent, Philo staggered back, barely keeping upright. With a last effort he kept his head from lolling. On the ground Wilson was still groaning, though his eyes were shut.

His head turned from one side to the other, a knee bent, as if his spirit were struggling to reanimate a rebellious body. Then he was still.

The crowd milled silently, awestruck about the battered figures.

'I knew he'd do it,' said Orville, grinning.

Panting, Philo sank to his knees at Wilson's side.

Wilson gasped and his eyes flickered open. 'Was I out?' he said.

Philo nodded, fighting for breath. 'Yeah.'

'How long?'

'Long enough,' Philo told him.

Wilson nodded, savouring the new experience. If he had to lose it was no shame to a man of Philo's talent. He shrugged. 'That's it then!'

'That's it,' grunted Philo.

His tight facial muscles stretched into the faintest grin; as the pain from his arm swelled with every breath he could manage no more.

He reached out his good arm to help Wilson to his feet. The movement broke the crowd's tension. There were cheers, light applause, laughter and congratulatory smiles from every side.

Philo smiled at Lynne in the crowd; relief was written all over her face.

'Man,' Fat Zack informed his party, 'That was one hell of a fight.'

As they nodded in agreement, Wilson slipped an arm round Philo's shoulder, part supporting him as they moved off through an aisle of applauding spectators.

'Better get that arm fixed,' he told his friend.

Sculking beyond the archway of steerhorns James Beekman turned away from the scene of jubilation with a sick look. 'I think we better get outta here,' he told Patrick Scarfe. Scarfe winced and slipped on a pair of dark glasses.

'I think you're right,' he said.

CHAPTER 15

Anthony Paoli Senior was a man who enjoyed his food.
Good Italian food with fine, full-bodied red wine. He'd
been most impressed by his glass at the restaurant that
afternoon. Pignatello, if he was any judge.

The Mafia wasn't the only useful thing to come out of
Sicily.

So it seemed perfectly natural to celebrate his vast
winnings at the very same restaurant this evening. True, it
was a little draughty with only a polythene sheet over the
space where the window had been. But the semolina
gnocchi alla Romana he was currently tucking into was
worth a small inconvenience. He glanced up as the beefier
of his two bodyguards joined him at his table. The man
was carrying a large attache case.

He opened it in front of his employer. Filling it were
neat rows of bank notes.

'He's payin' off thirty cents on the dollar,' the
bodyguard reported. 'Then he offered us forty cents, if we
promise not t' touch 'im.'

Mr Paoli grunted, chewing enthusiastically at his food.
He smacked his lips. 'Did you promise?' he asked.

'Of course,' said the other man.

Mr Paoli nodded, and swallowed. 'Right. Now go back
there an' – He speared another morsel of gnocchi and
popped it into his mouth ' – kill 'im.'

In marked contrast to the morning's mood, jollity reigned
in Fat Zack's re-booked hotel suite. Nothing could dim the
Texan's good humour, least of all the fact that he was
down to his vest and jockey shorts again and was
consistently drawing poor cards.

'Thirty cents on the dollar isn't gonna pay for the cost of
that plane,' said Little Melvin.

Zack shook his head and drew another card. 'It don't

matter,' he said, past his half smoked cigar. He chuckled. 'Hell, it's worth it t' pay for the privilege of seein' a fight like that.'

'Yeah ...' breathed Sweet Sue.

'Sure as hell is,' agreed Long John.

'Oh, I should say,' enthused the first of Zack's two guests. Kneeling beside her sister, the spinsterly lady in pink raised her eyes from her hand to see Zack beaming across the room at her.

His luck had just changed. 'I'm gonna have t' call ya on your bloomers, ma'am,' he drawled.

'Oh, *damn it*,' snapped the other. Then she flashed a totally disarming smile. 'Chivalry ain't dead in Texas.'

'Well, thank you, ma'am,' Zack grinned as the rest of the room broke up in laughter.

The atmosphere was more subdued two floors down in James Beekman's suite. Their luggage had already gone down to their hire car by the service lift at the back, at Beekman's insistence. It had been a painful afternoon; he'd been very fortunate to hang onto the fifty thousand he'd retained for expenses. He would have to keep a very low profile for a good six months, if not longer.

He shrugged on his jacket as Scarfe fitted the last of the fifty thousand into an attache case. He snapped it shut and handed it to his employer. He took a last glance round the room, then went to the door and opened it.

Anthony Paoli's bodyguards were leaving the elevator at the end of the corridor.

Scarfe slammed the door.

'What's the matter? Who is it?' Beekman snapped.

Scarfe swallowed. 'It's Tony's boys.'

'Tony's boys?' Beekman frowned. 'What're they comin' here for?'

'What the hell do you think they're comin' here for?' Scarfe hissed.

His eyes danced round the room, alighting on a curtain at the far end. He'd noticed a balcony beyond those curtains.

Beekman was still being dumb. 'Yeah, but they promised!' he wailed.

'Ohhh, Jesus ...!' Scarfe gasped in exasperation. He led the dash for the window.

In the corridor the tallest of the bodyguards knocked politely on the door. Glancing in either direction, his companion drew a heavy pistol from inside his jacket.

Mountaineering had never been Beekman's forte and the past decade of soft living had not increased his aptitude. Clinging to the side of the Ramada Snow King, he endured a five minute crash course only by telling himself he was more likely to survive a nasty fall than a bullet in the head.

Fortunately the modernistic design of the building gave it plenty of odd handholds. Climbing from balcony to balcony he only had to drop his own height into the darkness of a flowerbed.

'C'mon! C'mon!' he hissed at Scarfe.

Encumbered by the money case, Scarfe's progress was slower. He let the case fall, then pitched after it, grunting and staggering as he dropped at Beekman's feet.

'Hurry up!' Beekman whispered. 'Grab the case! C'mon!'

Glancing from left to right the two men scuttled out of the shadow of the building. The darkened forecourt looked deserted and the entrance lobby to their left showed no sign of Paoli's men.

Beekman spotted their hired limousine in a line of parked cars. Both men ran towards it. And drew up short as a group of dark figures rose from the shadows behind it.

The Widows had been waiting ever since Elmo and Woody had returned from Beekman's suite with considerably fewer winnings than they'd expected. Cholla knew he should have gone himself. But then desperadoes like the Black Widows always had another recourse when anyone was foolish enough to cross them.

Cholla swaggered forward into the light, rapping his riding crop across his palm. 'Hey, Beekman!' he smiled. 'I believe you owe us another seventy cents on the dollar!'

Beekman sighed, throwing a swift glance at the hotel entrance. 'C'mon!' he snapped. 'Get outta the way, you punks.'

Cholla rocked back on his jackboots with a look of affable indulgence.

'You really don't know who we are, do ya?' He turned to Woody. 'Tell 'im who we are!'

Woody pulled a half chewed cigar out of his mouth. 'We're the Black Widows,' he announced huskily. 'We're feared throughout the land.'

Cholla chuckled softly.

At that moment Paoli's bodyguards appeared at the hotel entrance. Looking round, they suddenly pointed at Scarfe and Beekman and began running in their direction.

Scarfe turned and saw them. 'Jim!' he cried.

Beekman gave them a swift glance. 'Let's get the hell outta here!' he wailed.

Both men turned and bolted - but not too quickly for Woody to snatch a large attaché case from Scarfe's hands. The Widows burst out laughing.

Elmo was ecstatic. 'You see how they lit outta here when they found out who we was!' he cackled.

'Didn't I tell ya I'd make ya great, huh?' roared Cholla.

The Widows nodded furiously - all but Dallas.

'Yeah, but we still got screwed, man!' he complained.

'Right, Dallas, we got screwed,' chimed in Frank.

Cholla's smile was tolerant. Leaning through the open window of Beekman's limo, he hooked out the keys on the end of his riding crop and held them up.

'Not quite,' he said. 'And I'd, uh, check that case, if I were you.'

He looked on, beaming, as Woody dropped the case on the bonnet and pulled it open. The Widows crowded behind him. Their eyes, like their mouths, grew steadily round.

To Philo, Orville and Clyde, Jackson's Million Dollar Cowboy Bar was the closest local equivalent to the Palomino: cool beer, dark-topped tables and familiar music from the clutered bandstand. Tonight's star was Glen Campbell, but Philo's party were still too engrossed in the events of the day to sit quietly and listen.

Philo let himself relax completely for the first time that day, for the first time in many days. Treated speedily as it was - with the help of Orville's new girlfriend - his arm still throbbed in its plaster cast and the beer was just beginning to take the edge off it.

'Well,' Orville announced, 'I got a telegram from Ma in Bakersfield. She's at another revival meetin'.'

Philo and Lynne grinned at the private joke. Orville's girlfriend, looking even more luscious to her beau out of uniform, flashed a questioning smile. Orville shook his head; Ma could come later.

Philo turned to Wilson. After all the agonies of their combat they both looked remarkably unmarked. As Wilson had once remarked, durability was a prime requisite of the bareknuckle battler.

'What're you gonna do? You gonna head back east?' Philo asked.

Wilson nodded. 'Yeah, I guess so.'

Philo took a swig from his beer. 'California ain't such a bad place.'

'Well, I'm not all that wild about it,' Wilson considered. Then he smiled at the company. 'But I do like the people. And the music is great.'

'Why thank you.' Lynne fluttered her eyelashes and made a mock bow.

'What about Beekman?' asked Philo. 'You gonna have any problems with him?'

Wilson took a deep breath. 'Uh, Beekman's the one with the problem,' he corrected. 'He can't cover the bets.'

Orville burst out laughing; it was welcome recompense for a crack on the head and a fine for dangerous driving, not to mention a bullet wound and several weeks of aggravation.

'Orville,' Philo said, 'wha'da ya say?'

Orville grew quieter. 'I'm stayin' in Jackson.' He grinned slyly at his girlfriend. 'For - uh - medical care.'

'Sure,' said Philo softly. He was grinning broadly.

'I love the place,' mimicked Lynne, 'and I looove the people!'

As Orville laughed and reddened, she ducked her head to Clyde and smacked her lips against his muzzle

'Ummm. Right, Clyde?'

The great ape gibbered and nuzzled her cheek.

Everybody laughed. The music swelled from the bandstand.

Philo and Lynne rose late at their motel the following morning. Making riotous love when Philo had one arm in a plaster cast and a host of inconveniently placed bruises had taxed their ingenuity well into the early hours. But they had several lost days to make up and their enthusiasm was boundless.

It was early afternoon before they rolled down Jackson's main street in the tow truck. Orville had bequeathed it – along with a few scribbled notes for Ma. His girlfriend had regaled him with tales of Jackson's massive tourist trade and Orville's eyes had widened at the prospect of limitless opportunity. There had to be something more profitable than his repair service racket.

Lynne pulled up at a crosswalk.

A long black convertible slid to a halt on Philo's side.

'Hey Beddoe!' cried a familiar voice.

Philo turned.

Cholla squatted high on the front seat headrest. Around him eight Black Widows were squeezed uncomfortably into the same machine. His eyes slitted in a look of bulky menace.

'You talkin' t' me?' Philo scowled.

'Yeah, I'm talkin' t' you!' Cholla snapped. 'We got a little debt t' settle!'

Philo felt Clyde stiffen beside him. 'We do, huh?'

Cholla's hand reached inside his leather coat. Suddenly his bloated face creased in a bountiful smile.

'Forty dollars!' he cried, drawing out a wad of bills and shoving them in Philo's direction. Uncertainly Philo

157

reached through the window and took them. 'Now I believe that makes us even,' Cholla beamed.

'I believe so,' said Philo warily.

'Ya know, Beddoe - ' Cholla plucked almost coyly at his riding crop. 'That was one hell of a fight you put up over there.' He looked at Philo squarely. 'I mean one *hell* of a fight.'

Philo nodded. 'I believe you boys had a little scuffle yourselves.' He was greeted with the unique and disconcerting sight of a host of bizarrely bewigged Widows grinning in embarrassed shyness.

'Yeah,' Cholla shook his head. 'It wasn't that bad.' The slight movement displaced his wig.

Philo glanced towards it and grunted.

'Oh.' Cholla straightened it, chuckling lightly. 'These things don't look bad when ya get 'em on straight.'

Beside him, Philo heard Lynne stifle a giggle. It was an effort to swallow his own laughter.

'No,' he assured Cholla, 'they look real good.' Cholla lavished the full benefit of his smile on Philo. 'You take care, Beddoe,' he told him.

Philo returned him the compliment. 'You do the same.'

Cholla slapped his crop against the side of the car. 'Let's go!' he yelled.

Accompanied by cheers and waves from the Widows, the overloaded vehicle lurched forward. As it drew away from the tow truck, three grinning members of the pack became visible in the open boot. They were holding a large cardboard sign, scrawled across it the words PHILO BEDDOE FOR PRESIDENT.

Laughing, Philo and Lynne heard Cholla's retreating cry. 'Are we rich motherssss!'

'We are rich motherssss!' the Widows bellowed in unison.

Lynne let go the brake, engaged first and headed for home.

A few miles out Clyde began to get restless. As Philo watched him, he rummaged under the seat and drew out a rolled up length of glossy paper. Carefully he unwrapped it and held it up.

It was a *Playboy* centrefold. Clyde smacked his lips and planted them on the paper.

'What do we have here?' Philo grinned. 'New girlfriend, Clyde?'

Lynne turned her gaze from the windshield, saw what it was and laughed.

'Very nice,' Philo agreed, 'but we may have trouble gettin' you this one.'

Clyde dropped the centrefold on the seat and groped under the dash.

He brought out a banana and Philo's animal syringe. He looked at Philo and raised his eyebrows.

'We'll do what we can, boy,' Philo told him.

They took the long way back, sticking to the state highways and the paved county roads, riding the busy freeways only when the country grew dull, which was rare. They travelled twisting mountain roads, past deep gorges and churning, white-frothed streams, small friendly hamlets and lonely hillsides of aspen and pine.

It was one of Philo's best times - beautiful in itself, but good in another way too. Though he nor Lynne never talked of it, it was a kind of reverse pilgrimage, re-making Philo's hopeful, bitter journey of the year before in vain pursuit of Lynne, re-making her flight, too, from him. Somehow this washed out all the unhappy memories, left them clean and whole and safe for the future.

It was late in the week when they finally crossed the Nevada border, slicing the length of Death Valley which Lynne had never seen before.

They were nearing the southern end close to noon with the empty highway and the emptier desert on either side shimmering in a hundred and twenty degrees of heat when the siren sounded. Philo glanced at Lynne with a frown. There was a motorcycle patrolman in the rear mirror.

They pulled over and waited as the CHiP man propped his bike and walked slowly up to the truck. He paused at

159

Lynne's window. Officer Morgan greeted them with a fierce grin.

'I thought I recognised you and your hairy friend!' he told Philo.

His expression changed abruptly. 'Cause of you, I'm stuck out here in this steam bath!'

He dragged his notebook out of his pocket and flipped it open.

'I'm citing you for speeding and reckless driving,' he said to Lynne.

'What!' Lynne gaped at him. 'We were only doing fifty!'

Ignoring her, Morgan walked round to the passenger window. Clyde gave him a baleful look.

'And I'm impounding this truck for evidence!' he snapped.

Philo stared at him. 'Impound it for what?'

Morgan stabbed a finger at Clyde. 'Evidence for transporting an animal without certificates of ownership - and certificates of innoculation.'

'Nobody owns Clyde,' said Philo. 'He's a free person.'

'The animal goes to the kennel,' Morgan barked, 'the truck goes to the police yard.' His eyes narrowed on Philo and blazed. 'I'm gonna be roastin' out in this desert for the next *three* years because of you, Beddoe. You're gonna pay!'

Philo turned to Lynne. She glanced back at Clyde. Then she gripped the steering wheel and gazed through the windshield.

'Right turn, Clyde,' she said.

The hairy fist shot through the open window with the force of a Beddoe blow. Morgan was out cold before he hit the sand.

Philo and Lynne exchanged smiles.

Clyde gave a hoot and gibbered happily. They were, Philo decided, a rare team.

He indicated the road ahead.

'Onward,' he ordered.